Don't Call It Paradise

Books by Gayle Pearson

Fish Friday

The Coming Home Cafe

One Potato, Tu

The Fog Doggies and Me

The Secret Box

Don't Call It Paradise

Don't Call It Paradise

GAYLE PEARSON

A Jean Karl Book

Atheneum Books for Young Readers

Atheneum Books for Young Readers
An imprint of Simon & Schuster Children's Publishing Division
1230 Avenue of the Americas
New York, New York 10020

Book design by Nina Barnett
The text of this book is set in Bembo.
Printed in the United States of America
10   9   8   7   6   5   4   3   2
Library of Congress Cataloging-in-Publication Data
Pearson, Gayle.
Don't call it paradise / Gayle Pearson.
p.   cm.
"A Jean Karl book."
Summary: When thirteen-year-old Maddie goes to visit her best friend Beanie
in California, she hopes that Beanie's older brother has changed, but she slowly
recalls a terrible secret from the past that makes her realize just what kind of
person he really is.
ISBN 0-689-82579-X
[1. Brothers and sisters—Fiction. 2. Friendship—Fiction. 3. Self-perception—
Fiction.] I. Title.
PZ7.P32312Do   1999   [Fic]—dc21   98-45338

For my father

ONE

AS SOON AS THE BIG 747 began its descent, those pesky old butterflies in the pit of my stomach took flight. I was no longer afraid of flying. I was no longer afraid of a lot of things. But I had this sudden panicky feeling that no one would be waiting for me at the gate. Or, worse yet, the McBeans would've sent Buddy to get me.

Swallowing hard, I turned my face toward the window, catching a fleeting glimpse of my suddenly somber reflection. Oh, lighten up, I thought, tucking a few wayward strands of dark blond hair behind my ears. So what if he is there. He was kind of a tough, crazy guy, but I was old enough to handle myself now. Then I took a deep breath and settled back into my seat.

The seat belt sign glowed a bright orange yellow. Just as I was tightening my belt, we hit an air pocket and the bottom dropped from under us. I clutched my *Seventeen* magazine with one hand and the armrest with the other, glancing at the faces of other passengers seated nearby. Nobody looked as though they were facing imminent death, so I didn't bother with a quick prayer. I really didn't think God would ruin my first trip to California with a plane crash.

And I knew the statistics were in my favor: that I was just as likely to die in a plane crash as I would be to choke to death on a balloon accidentally cooked into my hamburger in the school cafeteria.

Down below—and we were fast descending—the mountains, lakes, and wide-open spaces were being replaced by signs of civilization: buildings, stores, houses, highways, billboards. . . . Then, suddenly, a wide expanse of blue water burst into view. We were coming down low. I looked out at the plane's enormous wing as it dipped upward, then downward as we banked first to the left, then to the right. I crossed my fingers, a little throwback to the old me who worried about crashing. It looked like we should be landing, but all I saw beneath us was water, no runway! We were running out of room! Then . . . *bam* . . . *bam!* We were down. I opened my eyes as we zoomed down the runway, saw brown hills running along the horizon and a brilliant blue sky above it.

I shook my head to fluff up my hair and shoved my book into my carry-on bag. As I followed the long line of passengers through the tunnel that led to the terminal, I gripped my bag with nervous excitement and craned my neck. Then, suddenly, there was my best friend, Beanie, beaming and waving her arms. And beside her, her parents, Dennis and Marie. I bounded toward them, screeching— *eeeeeeeeeehhhhh*—like some sort of demented bird, as they swept me up into their giant embrace.

TWO

I'VE OFTEN WONDERED if it's possible to be born into the wrong family. I knew a girl in the sixth grade, Winnie Dillon, who was a musical genius born into a family whose other members were all tone-deaf. This was something I'd thought about ever since the McBeans moved into our neighborhood back when I was in the third grade and I started going over to their house after school to play with Beanie.

I remember the first time I walked through the McBeans' front door. It was not an ordinary house, and I knew it right away, perhaps because of the row of African tribal masks hung along one wall and the two giant cactus plants in big red pots made by Navajo Indians. My home was comfortable and I mostly didn't mind being there, but the McBeans' house was infinitely different. It crackled with energy, with ideas and opinions, with talk about travel and books, with music from Haiti and Brazil. We read the local newspapers at my house. The McBeans subscribed to the *New York Times.* My parents watched Wimbledon on TV. The McBeans belonged to a tennis club. At my house we ate well—meat loaf and spaghetti, roast chicken and grilled cheese sandwiches. But it was the McBeans who taught me that there is a difference between a red curry sauce and a green curry sauce and who gave me my first taste of espresso ice cream.

But the most amazing thing about the McBeans was this: When I walked through that door at the age of, what, eight or nine years old, the McBeans welcomed me with open arms and open hearts, as though I were a long-lost daughter. I never knew exactly why they did this, but I was happy and grateful. My life had been going along okay until then, but with the McBeans I suddenly felt reborn.

My parents said their moving away was in part because of Buddy—he was Beanie's older brother—some kind of trouble at school. You could've sent Buddy to Jupiter as far as I was concerned. I didn't like him because he was a show-off, an unbearable tease, and a perfect example of somebody being born into the wrong family. Oh, sure, I suppose there were times I kind of admired him for the reckless way he lived his life—but not very often. Maybe I blamed him for the McBeans' moving to California, too, and maybe he deserved it.

I truly didn't believe they were going until my parents drove them all to the airport on a terribly hot and humid day at the end of August last summer.

But that was then and this was now, and now we were all together again, zipping up and down the narrow hilly streets of San Francisco in the McBeans' cherry red Cherokee Jeep on our way to their home, about an hour north of the city. After an endless summer of waiting, waiting, and more waiting, I could hardly believe I was here.

"You two are sure going to have a lot to catch up on, aren't you?" said Beanie's mother, Marie, half turning in her seat to smile warmly in my direction. Marie could've been a talk show host. That's how pretty and smart she is.

I smiled back. Then, in a fake whisper, I leaned toward Beanie sitting beside me in the backseat and said, "Gee, that was smart of you, Beanie. Hiding all those monthly telephone bills so your parents wouldn't find them." She poked me on the shoulder, and we all cracked up.

I was only joking about the phone bills, of course. We wrote letters and exchanged a lot of E-mail. It wasn't the same though. Hard to laugh ourselves silly sitting in front of computers two thousand miles apart. Hard to fight and make up, hard to stay close. So I was relieved to see that Beanie hadn't turned into a totally different person in the past year. She looked pretty much the same as she had that awful day a year ago, when she'd waved good-bye to me from the backseat of my parents' blue Corolla as they pulled out of the McBeans' driveway just down the street (no room for me in the car).

Maybe she was a little taller, but not much—she had a ways to go to catch up with me. I'd shot up like a bamboo tree, as my mother proudly reminded me.

"So this is San Francisco. It looks more like a theme park than a city," I said, referring mostly to the cable cars clanging past us and our roller-coaster ride past row after row of the cutest little Victorian houses all fringed with gingerbread and painted in every color of the rainbow.

Beanie's father chuckled. He didn't seem to have changed much, either, except for a growing bald spot on the top of his head.

5

"It *is* a theme park and I'm the tour guide," he said. "You owe me ten bucks."

I laughed hard. The McBeans are witty. I loved that about them. My parents are nice. They are kind and even smart. But I wouldn't put them opposite the McBeans on a TV game show. I mean, my parents were the ones who *stayed* in the Midwest, where it was flat and boring, didn't they?

"Still the same funny Maddie," said Dennis, beaming at me in the rearview mirror. "Nice to see you've still got a good sense of humor."

I flushed with pleasure, always happy when the McBeans found me funny or smart. I looked down at my new blue-and-white sneakers. I looked at my scruffy jeans and my forest green windbreaker and the big watch on my left wrist. I smiled, because I knew I looked pretty cool. Yeah, I was still funny as ever, but I was almost fourteen and I knew that in a lot of ways I was changing.

The two hours it took to get from the airport south of the city to the McBeans' place out in the country north of San Francisco went by in a flash. A drive like that with my family would've been a different story—never something I looked forward to. My father hated driving. My mother liked to drive, but my father didn't like my mother's driving, and my mother hated that my father told her so. I was usually a captive in the backseat with my sister, Ginger, alternating between boredom and extreme irritation. Sometimes, to amuse myself, I would lean forward and watch my father, in the passenger seat, nearly drive his foot through the floor as he unconsciously tried to pump the spot on the floor where the brake should have been, or the gas pedal. He couldn't seem to help it.

The McBeans were not like that. They were a lot more relaxed. I sometimes wondered if how I used to be, so anxious and afraid of so many things, had something to do with growing up in a family of worriers. Was I eating too much sugar? Would the new welfare bill leave more people homeless? Had Dad hurt my feelings when he said this or that, and why were my left shoes wearing out faster than my right shoes?

"Buddy's sorry he couldn't make it," said Marie, half turning again in her seat up front.

"Huh?" I said, coming back into focus. Buddy was never sorry about anything, as far as I could remember, and I sure didn't see why he'd be sorry not to see me. I'd never much liked him, and we mostly kept our distance—I was Beanie's friend, not his.

"Oh, that's okay. We'll have plenty of time to catch up," I said, my head turned toward the window. I didn't dare look at Beanie. She knew how I felt about her brother, and she felt the same, only more so. Let's say he wasn't the sort of big brother a girl dreams about. He'd never taken Beanie "under his wing," the way you'd expect a big brother to do. No wings on this boy at all, not with the devil-may-care way he'd lived his life so far.

"I hope so," said Marie. "He's working tonight. Did Beanie mention he's got a job?"

She said this with a lot of enthusiasm. I shifted and squirmed in my seat. It was maybe the only thing I didn't admire about the McBeans, the way they seemed to dote on Buddy. I'd never understood it. And I felt sorry for Beanie. Their affection for her and Buddy had always seemed a little lopsided in his direction.

"I think so," I replied, glancing quickly at Beanie. She made a face and rolled her eyes. I shrugged. "Where's he working?"

"He buses tables at a little Mexican restaurant. He got the job in June for the summer, but he might stay on a few nights during the school year. If it works out."

"It'll work out," said Dennis. "Wait until you see him," he said, sounding proud. "Are you in for a big surprise!"

I hoped not. When it came to Buddy, a surprise was not a good thing.

"How about we take you there soon?" said Dennis, flashing me an eager smile in the rearview mirror. "Some night when he's working. Do you like Mexican?"

"I like to eat," I replied. This got some laughs all around, even from Beanie, who never seemed happy when the subject was Buddy. And who could blame her? He was a mean tease and he often hurt her feelings. I was just hoping that by now she was learning to stand up to Buddy's persecution, that the move to California would have given her a big shot of self-confidence.

"Wow!" I sat forward in my seat as we began to roll across the towering Golden Gate Bridge, thrilled down to my toes with my first-ever, up-close view of an ocean. Craning my neck, I could see dozens of sailboats dotting the bay to our right.

"Hey, Beanie," I said with a nudge to her shoulder. "Are you going to introduce me to any cute surfers, or what?"

"I think that's a subject we'd best save for the privacy of my room, don't you think?"

Her mother turned and gave us a look. "Which is where

you two will remain if you get any big ideas."

"That's nothing," said Dennis, pointing to a cluster of buildings on an island in the middle of the bay. "See that? That's Alcatraz. Used to be a big penitentiary way back when. Now it's used for girls who go boy crazy. So watch your step."

We cracked up. It was just like old times, and I couldn't have been happier.

I had no plans to go "boy crazy." Girls who did made me sick. But, let's say I met some cute guy at the beach one day, and he wanted to teach me how to windsurf. Let's say he looked half as good as the guy in the Coppertone ad on page 52 of the *Seventeen* magazine jammed into my duffel bag. Would I say no? No, I would not. I was sensible, but I was not stupid.

THREE

BEANIE'S FATHER KEPT A TIGHT GRIP on the Jeep's steering wheel as we bounced along the narrow, winding, rut-filled road that led to the McBeans' new house. I hung on to the Jeep's door handle, gazing out at the tall trees lining the road, already feeling envious of Beanie. She got to live in the country. I'd always wanted to live in the country. Then, as we pulled around the last curve in the road and their house came into full view, envy welled up inside me, pushing aside any other feelings I might have been having. I was speechless.

"Home sweet home," said Dennis, cutting the engine.

The house was splendid, sensational, the coolest place I'd ever seen. The first thing I spotted, perhaps because I so loved summer barbecues, was a big black barbecue grill set on a redwood deck. There were upper decks and lower decks, decks wrapped all around the house. It made the house resemble a ship, an ark come to rest on a small hill among towering trees. Late afternoon light danced off big rectangular windows.

"Shooooo . . . ," I exclaimed under my breath.

"Does that mean you like it?" asked Marie, popping her door open and sticking a leg out. "You think, if you try really hard, you'll be able to stand it here for a couple of weeks?"

I could feel Beanie smiling beside me. I wanted to be happy for her, and in a few seconds, when I was able to push the envy aside to make room, I would be.

"You lucky devil."

"I know," she replied. "It's neat, isn't it?" She began to fuss with her hair, twisting and pulling her unruly reddish brown curls through the hair band holding her ponytail in place.

"It's incredible," I gushed.

"We try to keep Beanie from falling all over herself with enthusiasm," her father commented wryly. "We don't want her to hurt herself getting carried away."

"Dad," said Beanie.

"That's right, *Dad*," said Marie, giving him a swat on the shoulder. "Button up. Everybody's different."

"You lucky devil." I sighed again. "Your parents bought a house that matches the color of your hair. Do you know how good that's going to look in all the photos? Shooooot . . . ," I said, shaking my head.

Then I flushed with embarrassment as the trunk slammed shut and Dennis came around the side of the car loaded down with my bags, a midsized one in each hand, and a small bag under his left arm.

"I tried to pack light, but . . ."

"Oh, I'm the same way," chuckled Marie. "Here, let me help."

I grabbed the small bag myself, then we turned toward the house. We were making our way single file up a small footpath when a big yellow dog suddenly bounded toward us, yelping its head off.

I was startled for a second, amazed by how much this dog looked like a dog Buddy had back in La Grange.

"Wow! She looks just like Mambo!" I blurted, dropping my bag.

"Yeah, poor Mambo," huffed Dennis from the back of the pack. "Hula, sit!"

"Hula, sit!" repeated Beanie rather fiercely, grabbing Hula by the collar and hanging on until she did sit. "Maddie, this is Hula! Hula, do you want to shake hands?" Hula didn't. She wanted to kiss me instead, springing to her feet and making a wild leap for my face with a long rosy pink tongue the color of Play-Doh.

"Sorry, Maddie," said Dennis. "She loves company and gets a bit carried away."

"It's really okay. I don't mind at all. Look how friendly she is." I dropped to my knees and gave her a smack on the nose—you can do that with golden retrievers—running my hands through her thick golden mane. "We're friends already, aren't we, Hula? Aren't we, girl?" She squealed with delight, running her tongue up and down my chin. It's hard to tell some golden retrievers apart, but the resemblance to poor Mambo was uncanny. In fact, as I gazed for a second or two into her big black dog eyes, I felt suddenly pulled backward in time, as though I really were gazing into the eyes of Mambo, or the ghost of poor Mambo.

I quickly got to my feet.

But Hula wasn't done with me. She suddenly rose up on her hind legs, placing her front paws heavily on my chest.

"More kissy face, Hula? Aren't you a sweetie?"

"Gee, look how much she likes you," said Beanie.

"You know me," I replied matter-of-factly, "immensely popular with dogs and mosquitoes."

As Hula led the way up to the McBeans' new house, I let myself think about Mambo for the first time in ages. Though I'd never cared much for Buddy, I did love his dog, a large golden retriever with a heart as big as the sky. I'd always figured that a boy who had a dog that good couldn't be all that bad. But the poor dog drowned when she was only three years old.

I called my parents before dinner, as promised, to tell them I'd arrived safely. It felt really funny to talk with them, knowing I was a few thousand miles away, and I did have a flash of homesickness, but only for a few seconds. Mostly I felt sorry for them. *They* sounded homesick, not me.

It was 7:30 P.M. in La Grange, 5:30 P.M. in California. That was something I'd never understood, how it could be one time in one place and another time someplace else. Time ought to be a fixed thing, like space. It ought to be one way or the other, like a lie versus the truth.

By 9:30 California time, I'd begun to fall asleep in the middle of my sentences, so I bid everyone a good night and went up to bed. Beanie came with me.

"Beanie?"

"Yeah?"

I wriggled my bare toes under the cool bedsheets and yawned.

"Hula seems like a great dog."

"She is a great dog."

I had this uneasy feeling, like there should be more to say on the subject, but I couldn't think of a thing, so I let it drop, quietly surveying the contents of Beanie's room in the dim light instead. Surprisingly, it looked almost exactly the way it had back in Illinois. Same posters on the walls, same stuff on top of her dresser—jewelry box, bowl of barrettes, fossilized rocks, ceramic horses . . .—rearranged in exactly the way it'd always been. I thought it was odd. If it were me, I would've changed everything! I would've wanted my new room to look totally different, not the same as it'd always been.

"Why didn't you tell me your brother had a job?"

"I don't know. I thought I had."

"Must be a big relief to have him gone so much. Your parents seem really proud of him."

"My parents would be proud if he hung from the trees by his toes."

I laughed. She was right, though, and I never could quite understand it.

"Same ol' Buddy?" I said.

"Same ol' Buddy," she repeated. "And my parents are as ignorant as ever. They're into birds now. They've each got a pair of binoculars, which is really hysterical, since they can't see what's going on right under their own noses."

It was hard for me to take what she was saying very seriously. Dennis and Marie were so cool, they'd make the top of most kids' lists of Ideal Parents. I'd always been envious, but I supposed nobody was perfect, not even the McBeans.

"Beanie. How long does it take you to drive to the ocean from here?"

"Twenty minutes. Why?"

"Whoever would have thought it, you living so close to the ocean like this? After all those summers swimming in that filthy quarry."

"It wasn't so bad."

"No, it wasn't. We had a lot of good times, didn't we?"

"Oh, Maddie," she suddenly blurted. "I'm so glad you're here! I've missed you so much!"

"Me, too!" I reached across the space between the beds and grabbed Beanie's hand, squeezing it hard. A few seconds later, her hand grew limp.

"Beanie?"

No answer.

"Beanie?"

She'd always been like that, awake one minute and dead asleep the next.

"Night, Beanie," I said, then rolled over, figuring I'd fall asleep immediately myself, but I didn't. I was wide awake thinking about what Beanie had said about her parents. Who doesn't get sick and tired of their own family? I thought. Me, I was sure glad to get away from mine. I'd had it with my little sister, Ginger, tailing me from room to room with a zillion questions and comments, was sick of the sound of my dad chipping golf balls in the yard. *Pop. Pop. Pop.* Sick of my mom asking if I'd put away the dishes and fed the dog.

I was ready for something different, and I was pretty sure it was going to happen. I didn't think it was just hope that was making me feel that way, either. I'd seen enough movies and heard enough stories about things that happened to people on vacation to figure there was a good chance something could happen to me.

I was facing the wall, and now I looked up into the big blown-up face of Robbie Robin, lead singer for Banana Rex. He was pretty cool, but nobody I'd go nuts over—and certainly not as cute as the guy carrying a kayak on page 76 of my *Seventeen* magazine. It was an old poster, of course, and I marveled again as to why Beanie would want to have all her stuff the way it had been back in La Grange. I suddenly wondered if Beanie had a boyfriend, then dismissed the idea as soon as it entered my mind. I was sure she would've told me.

Every so often I could hear stuff from the living room downstairs, the voices of Dennis and Marie mixing in with people talking on television. I thought about my own parents, a couple of thousand miles away, maybe having a late-night snack while watching TV. Their routine didn't vary much, and I was glad I was here and not there. I was never bored with the McBeans. And I was sure if they knew how Buddy tormented his sister, they would've done something about it a long time ago.

I awoke with a start sometime in the middle of the night, my heart pounding furiously in my chest. I sat up on my elbows and looked around, wondering where in the world I was. The light and shadows cascading across the walls and the ceiling were all wrong, unfamiliar. Then I saw Beanie asleep in the twin bed next to mine and sighed with relief. Right about that time I heard the sound of heavy footsteps on the stairway, then on the wooden floor of the hallway outside Beanie's room. Somehow I knew it was Buddy. I also heard a soft dull *tap tap tap* and a little clicking sound. What was *that?* I wondered, gazing at the shadowy shapes quivering above me on the ceiling. Then I realized it was the sound of Hula's paws and toenails hitting the hardwood floor as she followed Buddy down the hallway to his room. A door opened, then closed.

I lay back down with a shiver—nights in California were chillier than I'd expected—and pulled the cover up to my chin. Somewhere deep down inside me, I knew that something bad had happened a long time ago. Then, with a chill that shot from my neck to my spine, I had an overwhelming sense that I was somehow involved, that it had something to do with Buddy and Mambo and me. It was only a kernel of a memory, nothing to latch on to, and I didn't even want to try. I was here on vacation. Let sleeping dogs lie, as the old saying went.

But I shivered again—and not from the cold.

FOUR

BUDDY WAS STILL ASLEEP when the rest of us took off for the beach early Saturday morning. But Hula wasn't. She squealed and wiggled her butt with delight as soon as the beach bags and beach blankets were hauled from the downstairs closet.

I hadn't quite shaken the creepy feelings I'd had in the middle of the night. It wasn't any way to start a vacation, but going to the beach really was. I'd never been to the ocean. Back in La Grange, it was a big deal to drive in to one of the beaches along Lake Michigan, and we almost never did. Instead we spent long summer days at the La Grange community pool about a mile from my house or at the abandoned quarry out near the forest preserve.

Dennis and Marie took us to a place called Drake's Beach inside the Point Reyes National Seashore. Every so often, in the middle of chasing the Frisbee with Hula, I had to stop what I was doing and just look. This is the Pacific Ocean, I would say to myself. The *Pacific Ocean*.

"Sorry!" Beanie hollered, as I leaped for the Frisbee about to sail over my head. Beanie had many wonderful qualities, but athletic coordination was not one of them. She couldn't catch and she couldn't throw. Lucky for me that Hula came along with us that day. She sprinted past me with glee and returned in a few seconds with Frisbee in mouth.

I'd always felt sorry for Beanie in PE. Everybody liked her, but nobody wanted to pick her. She was not only clumsy, but afraid of the ball. She'd back away from pitches in the strike zone, swinging instead at pitches so far out you couldn't hit them with the trunk of a tree. Forget about fighting for the basketball under the net or diving for a spiked ball in volley-ball. But if ever I was the captain and had to choose, I always chose her. So what if we lost. She was my best friend, and I wasn't going to let her stand there with her head hanging down, feeling bad because she wasn't good at something. Not for two seconds I wouldn't.

"You didn't have to pick me," she'd say later, "just because we're friends. I know I'm a crummy ballplayer."

"I picked you for your enthusiasm and your great spirit," I'd say. "They're just as important as anything." And this I truly believed.

"Nice throw!" I hollered to Beanie, as the Frisbee sailed right for my navel. I watched, though, amazed, as it suddenly veered toward my right, landing thirty feet out in the ocean.

She lifted her shoulders in a shrug.

"Well, nice curveball," I said. "I'm hot anyway." Then I waded carefully out into the icy water, trying to set my feet down on soft sandy spots on the ocean floor. Between the rocky bottom and the temperature of the water, I could sure see why more people weren't swimming. It was tough going, and I was concerned about losing the Frisbee, but Hula suddenly darted past me and was soon dog-paddling her way back to shore, Frisbee in mouth.

I waved to Beanie. She was laughing. I suppose I looked funny as I tried to get out of the water. I'd make a few feet of progress then get pulled back by waves receding from shore. I started laughing, too, which of course affected my coordination, slowing my progress even further. The harder I laughed, the weaker I seemed to get, and I was already tired. Then, *bam!* A huge wave hit me from behind and down I went, suddenly swept onto my hands and knees, the water rushing over me. Staggering to my feet, I fought to stay standing as the water swirled about my knees on its way back out to sea.

Dennis and Marie had been perched side by side on a square plaid blanket set a ways back up on the sand. Dennis was standing now, and suddenly I realized they were both looking at me.

I raised my arm and was about to wave, at which point I was clobbered from behind by another little whitecap. Down I went and down I stayed, crawling my way back to shore. I was happy to finally get there but embarrassed to have the McBeans see me flopping around like a clumsy sea lion, then heaving myself up onto shore like a beached whale.

Beanie was bent over double, laughing her head off.

I sat up slowly, pulling a stringy piece of seaweed from my hair.

"Are you all right?" asked Dennis, gazing down at me with his hands on his hips.

"Yeah . . . I'm fine. Where's the resuscitator?"

He extended his hand and pulled me to my feet. "You

20

had us worried. Be careful out here, Madison. It's not Lake Michigan, you know."

"I know. It's freezing, for one thing."

Marie helped brush the sand from my shoulders and back. I pulled another slimy strand of seaweed from around my ankle as the four of us strolled toward the blanket.

"People eat that stuff here," said Beanie. "They collect it and take it home and put it in a big pot and boil it. It's supposed to be good for you."

"Is that right?" I said, still breathing hard. "Well, I think I'll stick to spinach if it's all right with you."

"Gee, a whole pot of seaweed gone to waste," said Marie. "Now we've got nothing for dinner."

This was something else I appreciated about the McBeans. They didn't get all worked up about nothing. They didn't launch into lectures when a little something went wrong. My own father *would've* been out there with a resuscitator. I would've heard about it for days, maybe weeks. When I was three years old, they tied me to a tree in front of a cottage they'd rented so I wouldn't wander down to the lake and drown. Imagine *that* being your first vacation experience.

"There's an old saying," said Dennis, tugging at the corners of the blanket to even it out. "And I think it's one you should listen to. It says you should never turn your back on the sea."

"Really?" I asked, brushing the sand from the bottom of my feet before plopping down. "Why?"

"Sleeper waves," he said ominously.

"Sleeper waves," I repeated. "In terry cloth bathrobes."

21

This cracked everyone up. I threw myself facedown on the blanket, cradling my head in my arm. The sun felt deliciously hot on my back, but if I were at home, my mother would be tossing me the sunscreen. "Here, babe, cover yourself up." So much for a suntan. But not this time, not here in Paradise.

"It's Dennis's sneaky way to tell you two to be careful out here," said Marie. "We don't want anything to happen to you."

"Okay," I replied simply. "We will." And that was that. No lecture, no big production. I felt a nudge on my shoulder and lifted my head. It was Hula, poking me with the Frisbee, her eyes begging me to keep playing.

"Whew, I'm beat, girl. I'll have to take a rain check. Sorry."

Looking past her, I saw a guy with a girl in a yellow bikini lying side by side on a blanket up near some tall grasses in a little cove. I wondered if her boyfriend liked her bikini, and I wondered what they were laughing about.

Hula dropped the Frisbee in the sand right in front of me and now sat gazing down at it intently, as though she were trying to levitate it right off the ground. Or levitate me.

"I know you want to play, Hula, but I'm tired. Let's take a little rest, okay?" You could see everything right in her eyes. Longing, disappointment, understanding. I lifted my arm and rubbed her nose. And, with a twinge of sadness, I thought about Mambo again.

I lowered my head into the crook of my arm. Little bursts of colored light flickered before my eyes, as sometimes happens when you've been staring into the sun. Then I saw a picture of the quarry back in La Grange and heard a small voice saying, *Remember the quarry. Don't forget about the quarry.* Though the sun was sizzling my back and legs, a shiver ran the length of my body, as it had when I'd awakened in the middle of the night.

I lifted my head and picked up the Frisbee. Then I sent it flying, watching as it sailed upward, a mini saucer against a perfectly blue California sky. *Let sleeping dogs lie,* I silently insisted again. I wasn't sure what that old saying meant, but it seemed to fit the new person I was working hard to be. Somebody who didn't worry about every little thing, a strong and fun-loving girl who was looking toward the future, not the past.

Hula spurted after the Frisbee. I turned my head to avoid a face full of sand. The girl in the bikini pointed a squirt gun at her boyfriend. I looked down at my blue swimsuit, the first two-piece I'd ever owned, and tried to see it through his eyes.

I had an urge to grab the binoculars from Marie's hands to get a closer look, but of course I didn't. "See anything interesting?" I asked her.

"Oh, there's always something to look at," she replied. "I'd love to catch sight of an auklet. That would be super."

"What's an auklet?" I asked.

"A rhinoceros auklet is like a puffin, only a much rarer bird," said Dennis. "Point Reyes is a great place for bird-watching, you know."

"I'm a rare bird!" I blurted.

Dennis and Marie roared.

In the past I might have also hopped to my feet and done

a crazy little chicken dance, waddling pigeon-toed around in the sand. But I held myself back. I was still seeing myself through the eyes of the guy with the girl in the yellow bikini, and I didn't think he'd go for a chicken dance at all. I turned to check them out again, just to see what they were up to now. They were kissing, and I quickly looked away.

I have this picture in my mind. It's of me and Beanie, Dennis and Marie sitting cross-legged in a circle on the beach. It's early afternoon, and we have a little picnic spread out before us on the blanket. We're gobbling up the turkey sandwiches, chips, fruit, and macadamia-nut cookies like there's no tomorrow. We're tired because we went for a long walk on the beach and for a swim in the icy water, but we feel so happy together. It's not just me. We've all said so. Everything seems perfect. It's a snapshot I'll always have with me.

That night, after a stop at home to clean up, we surprised Buddy with an unplanned visit to El Gordo's for dinner.

Who was more surprised, Buddy or me?

Basically, in a nutshell, Buddy was hot, wicked hot, not the Buddy I remembered at all.

I was studying the menu, about the size of a small telephone book, when I happened to glance at this guy carrying a tray of dirty dishes across the room. This guy, in a short-sleeved white shirt and khaki pants, was *cute*. Longish brown hair, dark eyes, great tan. I didn't realize it was Buddy until Marie waved him over. He'd shot up like a weed, so he was still a bit on the thin side, but you could already tell. This guy was going to be stunning, drop-dead gorgeous.

You could've knocked me over with a nacho.

Coming over to my side of the table, he set the tray of dishes down and gave me a playful poke on the shoulder. "Hey, welcome to crazy California. Gee, Madison. You look great. I wouldn't have recognized you."

Ditto, I said to myself. But in reality I was tongue-tied. I couldn't think of anything clever or interesting to say. "Th ... thanks," I stumbled, twisting my napkin in my lap like an idiot.

"See, she is surprised," said Dennis, nodding in my direction. "We told her you'd changed, but she had to see it for herself."

"Have I changed?" asked Buddy, sounding incredulous. He held his hands up in front of his face. "Nope, looks like the same old me."

I laughed along with Dennis and Marie.

"It's the same ol' you all right," mumbled Beanie.

"Beanie," cautioned her mother.

"Brothers and sisters." Dennis sighed. "I was the same way with mine." He smiled. I smiled back to let him know I understood.

"Well, catch you later," said Buddy. "Maybe a bike ride tomorrow?"

"Sure." I nodded and smiled. Dopey answer, I thought, pinching myself under the table.

Knockdown, drop-dead gorgeous, and a smile to go with it. I watched as he disappeared through the swinging doors into the kitchen a few moments later, then turned to Dennis and Marie.

"I see what you mean. He sure does look great."

I snuck a sideways glance at Beanie, lifting my eyebrows in surprise. *Same ol' Buddy?* Was she crazy or what?

"Yep, California's been good for him," said a beaming Marie. "It's been good for us all. Isn't that right, Beanie?"

"If you say so." She shrugged.

Marie sighed and picked up her menu.

I read the sigh to mean *Gee, we just can't seem to please her.*

I didn't know what to say and lifted my menu, too. In spite of the awkwardness of the moment, I felt sort of giddy. In fact, I felt like laughing out loud. Buddy McBean. The joke was on me.

"Beanie," I said cheerily, "see where it says *chimichanga* on the menu?"

"Yeah?"

"Is that a dance or something to eat?"

She giggled, finally lowering her menu to shake her head and grin.

I ordered the chimichangas, not because I liked chimichangas. I didn't know the first thing about them. And that's why I ordered them. I'd never had them before. I was happy. Happy made me feel bold and adventurous, ready to try something new.

FIVE

I FUMBLED AROUND the second drawer of the dresser for a plain yellow T-shirt to go with my navy blue shorts. I wanted to look nice, but not too nice. Buddy had mentioned going on a bike ride again over breakfast that morning. He still seemed sweet, still was great looking, and I still couldn't get over the new Buddy.

"I think we should go and give your brother a chance," I said to Beanie. "It seems like he's trying to change . . . Well, he obviously already has changed. In fact, I really can't get over it." I was trying to talk her into going—I knew I wouldn't go without her—and not having a whole lot of luck. She was lying on her back on her bed, gazing dejectedly up at the ceiling.

"I think you should go with an open mind," I added. I pulled out the yellow T-shirt and a pair of clean white socks. "That's what I'm doing. And you know how I've always felt about Buddy. If I can do it, you can do it. What do you say?"

"You can't be serious," muttered Beanie.

"Well, I guess I am. *I* can see he's changed; your *parents* can see he's changed. Maybe you're just stuck in the past." I heard the pitch of my voice rising and knew I was in danger of overstating my case. If I pushed Beanie too fast or too hard, it would backfire. She'd never budge, never even get up off the bed.

"Looks aren't everything," said Beanie. "He's taller and tanner, and that's about the extent of it."

"Oh, Beanie. That's so lame. I'm not just talking about looks at all. I'm talking about the way he acted. Besides, we're only going on a little bike ride here, not off to the Grand Canyon."

"I know. I just don't enjoy hanging out with him."

"I know you don't." I slipped the T-shirt on over my head, allowing myself a quick scowl of frustration. I was eager to get going, and I didn't want to waste a beautiful day. But I also knew why Beanie felt like she did, and I couldn't really blame her.

"Look, Beanie." I sat down on the edge of her bed. "I know Buddy's made your life pretty miserable. But people really do change, and I see some sign of hope here. I could be wrong, but there's only one way to find out—do things with him and see. Maybe Buddy's finally growing up. What is he, sixteen now? Anyway, if he's nice enough to offer to take us on a bike ride, I think we should go."

"*Nice* is not a word I'd use to describe him," she muttered. "Besides, I ate too much. I'm not sure I can ride on a full stomach."

"We all ate too much. That's not a good reason."

We'd just come up from breakfast. We're not talking Cheerios here. We're not even talking bacon and eggs. Marie'd whipped up a batch of her famous blue germ pancakes, loaded with blueberries and wheat germ and served with real maple syrup from Vermont.

Beanie finally pulled herself up off the bed, then skulked about the room for a while before reluctantly agreeing to go. I knew she was only going because she didn't want to disappoint me. I suppose you could say I sometimes got my own way because she didn't have a selfish bone in her body. I'd rather she were going because *she* wanted to, of course, but sometimes you have to take what comes your way.

Besides, I had my own concerns about going riding with a guy who used to turn walking down the street into a big competition. As I tightened the laces on each of my sneakers with a little snap, I remembered the bicycle jump he'd set up with Danny Ruda years ago. I'd watched from the sidelines as they rode their bikes off the ledge of a small hill, then over a couple of garbage cans laid end to end. Danny broke his collarbone. Nothing ever happened to Buddy. He seemed a little crazy to me, like a character you'd see in a movie. The guy had guts though. You had to give him something for that, though I wasn't sure what. Maybe ten years in the U.S. Marines.

"I guess I just hate to share you," said Beanie, grabbing a barrette from the top of her dresser. "Especially with him, and especially since you just got here."

"It's just a bike ride," I said, as I saw myself sailing over a pile of old garbage cans. "We're just taking advantage of his expertise, and we'll have tons of time together, just the two of us. Okay?"

By the time we made it downstairs, Buddy had three bicycles—his, Beanie's, and one Marie sometimes rode—lined up alongside the house, ready to go. I waved good-bye to Marie and Dennis, who were out on the deck drinking coffee as we rode away. (I *loved* coffee, and the McBeans usually let me have some!)

Beanie and I followed Buddy on our bikes down the long unpaved driveway that led to the main road, me with an open mind and open heart, Beanie's open-heartedness about the size of a pea. We stayed on the main road for five minutes or so, then turned off onto a fire road.

Riding uphill was hard work, and I was soon out of breath. I'd never done much pedaling uphill, mainly because there wasn't much uphill to pedal back in Illinois. And I have to admit that with Buddy right behind me, I was awfully nervous. I wondered if he thought I was going too slow, but I tried to go faster and just couldn't. A couple of those large blue germ pancakes were still trying to find a home in the pit of my stomach.

"Hey, Beanie . . . !" I gasped, unable to finish the sentence.

She turned to give me this agonized look, and I thought, with some guilt, Oh good. I wasn't the only one suffering. Her face was flushed a bright red—like a pinto bean—and she was panting. It was funny. I wanted to crack up but didn't. We were both heaving and gasping like old horses.

Along this stretch of the road, the trees loomed tall on either side. It was pretty. The air was full of a piney smell, but if I followed Beanie too closely, I got a face full of dust and couldn't smell anything.

Suddenly Buddy sped by me. He seemed to do it with no effort at all. "Catch you later!" he hollered, then flew past Beanie as well.

"Not if I catch you first!" I croaked back, then cringed

when I heard myself say it. I'd have to do better than that.

Buddy led us off the fire road onto a narrower trail, so narrow that the low-lying bushes and scrubby undergrowth crowding in close scratched up my bare legs. Twigs, branches, and leaves crackled and snapped under the bicycle's fat off-road tires, which bounced over tree roots stretched across the road like fat snakes. My legs were aching, and I wasn't sure I could go much farther, but I much preferred what I was doing to a typical Sunday morning back home.

Not counting for the difference in time, I'd be slumped over the comics at the kitchen table, working my way through a bowl of Rice Krispies. At that very moment, my dad was probably concentrating on frying those eggs just right, keeping the yolks from breaking, and my mom would be sipping her coffee, reading bits and pieces of some news-paper article out loud, and he'd be saying, "Yeah, uh-huh, uh-huh, is that right?" Then church, then dinner, same old thing, same old thing every Sunday. I was lucky to be here!

I wondered if they missed me.

"It's too steep!" I heard Beanie croak. It sure is, I silently agreed, but I would never have said so out loud, not around Buddy. Instead I just kept pushing down on the pedals with everything I had, hoping and praying it wasn't much farther to the top.

Just when I thought I couldn't pedal another foot, the trail suddenly leveled off. Sweat dripped from my face as we coasted along the flat stretch. My T-shirt felt like a piece of Saran Wrap stuck to my back.

Up ahead I heard Beanie holler for Buddy to stop, but he seemed to speed up instead, disappearing around a turn up the road. I figured we'd try to catch up to him, but Beanie sent her bike into a skid instead, dragging her left foot along the ground until the bike came to a complete stop.

"What's up?" I said, gradually gliding to a stop beside her.

"See? You heard me ask him to stop, didn't you? But where is he? He's way up ahead of us now. I need water. I'm dying of thirst, and I'm not going to pedal another . . ."

"I don't think he heard you, Beanie. He was a ways ahead of us already. See, here he comes." Beanie could be a stubborn mule, and when she said she wouldn't move an inch, she meant it. Me, I was kind of embarrassed to be just standing there in the middle of the road like that, with Buddy having to come back and get us, even though I was dying of thirst myself.

"You two aren't quitting on me, are you?" he hollered, hardly breathing hard at all as he slowly pedaled his way back toward us.

"No, but we will if we don't get some water!" shouted Beanie.

"Hey, I'm not quitting! Speak for yourself," I croaked. My mouth was so dry I could barely speak, but I wanted to make sure Buddy knew I wasn't a quitter. I'd always been proud of my athletic ability, but I had to admit that, so far, this was a bit more than I'd bargained for.

"You doing okay?" he asked, pulling up alongside me. He handed me a plastic water bottle, and I had to hold myself back from chugging the whole thing. This new Buddy was so sweet and every bit as cute as the night before.

I nodded, hoping my face wasn't too red from exertion. "I guess I'm holding my own. I just haven't done much . . ."

I had to stop and take a breath. The hair around his forehead and ears looked curly and damp, and I was glad to see that he'd worked up a sweat.

". . . much uphill riding," I continued. "You know, not very hilly back in La Grange."

"Yep. Flat as an ironing board. Well, you're doing great, really hanging in there . . ."

I was hoping he'd say something nice and encouraging to Beanie now, too, but he didn't have much of a chance before Beanie cut in.

"How much farther do we have to go? You said this was a short, easy ride."

"I said pretty easy," Buddy replied evenly.

I could see she was testing his patience, and you could hardly blame him. She was testing mine, too.

"We're at the top, so the hardest part's over." He wiped his face on the sleeve of his shirt. I noticed the muscles in his calves and thighs. They were enormous. I had to stop myself from staring.

"Well, you guys ready?" He slipped the water bottle back in a pouch behind the seat of his bike and shoved off with his right foot. "You know the saying," he added with a little smirk, "'What goes up, must always come down.'" And away he went.

I looked at Beanie. "Let's go."

She rolled her eyes. "Mr. Einstein," she mumbled. "As if he's the brain in the family."

"He sure is a good rider," I said.

"Huh," she replied.

The descent was gradual at first, nothing to it. You just

had to hang on and enjoy the ride. Then, suddenly, the road seemed to drop away altogether and down we went, plunging forward at an incredible angle and speed. "Whoooooaa . . ." I heard myself pleading, as I found myself pitching forward, nearly somersaulting over the handlebars. "Whooooooaaa . . ."

We were really flying. I couldn't keep my feet on the pedals, so forget trying to do any braking. The only thing that kept me and the bike from separating altogether was my white-knuckle death grip on the handlebars. I couldn't see Beanie, just a cloud of dust up ahead, but I could hear her screaming. I didn't want to scream, not with Buddy within earshot. So I gritted my teeth and hung on, tears stinging my eyes from the wind. If I'd been on a roller coaster—and it was a lot like that—I would've closed my eyes until it was over.

Suddenly the trees slid away, the trail leveled off, and we were flying single file, still on the trail but through a wide meadow. Skidding off into the brown grassy meadow itself, Buddy suddenly broke out of the formation. As Beanie and I flew past him, I saw him grinning out of the corner of my eye. I sure hoped he wasn't getting his kicks at our expense. That would've been too much like the old Buddy, and a big disappointment.

And now here was Beanie, trying to follow her brother's lead in a skid off the trail and into the meadow. She pulled into a skid all right, but as I flew past her, I saw her bike twist out of control, slipping and sliding like crazy, until it finally sent her hurtling into a dense thicket at the meadow's edge.

I was going too fast myself to stop and hop off, so I put the brakes on gradually, then turned without stopping and sped back up the trail.

Poor Beanie. What a sight. She was kneeling beside her

bicycle, picking leaves and twigs from her hair. I was sort of surprised Buddy hadn't got off his own bike to help her, but when I heard her yelling at him, I could understand why.

"I could've been hurt, Buddy!" she blurted miserably. "You never think about anybody but yourself!" Her face was blotchy and red and I knew she was trying to keep it together. She hated to cry in front of her brother.

"Don't worry. She's not hurt," he mumbled wearily, still perched on the seat of his bike.

I scrambled off mine, laying it flat in the grass. "Oh, good," I awkwardly mumbled, feeling as though I ought to apologize for going to help her.

I tried to rush without being obvious, covering the distance between Beanie and me with very long strides.

"You okay?" I asked, grasping Beanie by the hand and pulling her up onto her feet.

"Basically. But I went right over the handlebars. I could've been killed."

"Well, I don't know about *that*, but I'm glad you're okay."

"No, she's right," Buddy scoffed. "Those bushes are really tough, like running into a block of granite."

"We were going too fast and you know it!" she hollered. She swatted the seat of her pants, which emitted a small cloud of dust.

"You're *okay*, Beanie, or you wouldn't be up and moving. Trust me. You're just a bit shaken up."

"Who wouldn't be!"

Buddy looked at me and shrugged, shaking his head. I can't help it if she's like this, he seemed to be saying.

I pressed my lips together, trying for as slight a shrug in

return as I could manage. I didn't want it to seem like I was on his side, and I sure didn't want to smile and hurt Beanie's feelings. I was feeling bad enough as it was. It was my idea to come, after all, and look at the poor girl now.

"You've still got a twig in your hair, right above your left ear. Here, let me get it," I offered.

"Thanks," she murmured. She still had tears in her eyes, and this, I have to say, surprised me. It seemed like the kind of thing we would've just laughed about back in La Grange.

"Are you sure you're okay?"

"Yeah, I just want to get home."

So did I by this time. What I didn't want was to get caught in the middle of a fight between her and Buddy. I'd been there before, and I hadn't liked it a bit.

"If anything's wrong with me, you're in for it, Buddy, and you know it." Beanie grabbed her bike by the handlebars and gave it a shake. A few dead leaves fell from the spokes of the front wheel.

"There is something wrong with you, Beanie. A set of training wheels should help, though."

It was kind of a mean thing to say, but the old bad-mouth Buddy would've said something worse.

"Darn you, and thanks for the death ride!" snapped Beanie. She threw her leg over the crossbar and climbed on.

"*Death ride?*" Buddy laughed, shaking his head. "Oh, Beanie, sometimes you're way out in left field, you know?"

I felt a little like laughing myself, but I squelched it. Instead I got back onto my bike and got ready to go.

"All set?" asked Buddy.

"How'd *you* like the death ride?" asked Beanie, suddenly

turning to me. "Go ahead, tell the truth!"

I blushed, pressing my lips together and squinting at the sun-parched earth beneath my feet. Did I look like a referee? Well, I didn't want to be one, so I searched my mind for the right thing to say. It *was* a rough ride, and yet I *had* enjoyed it. But no, I didn't think it was the right ride for Beanie, and I think Buddy knew it. *Brothers and sisters*, I heard Dennis say. Well, maybe.

Wiping the sweat from my face and neck, I lifted my head to look at a hawk circling above us.

"You've put Maddie on the spot," said Buddy. "Look how she's perspiring from all the pressure."

"Oh, I'm all right," I objected.

"Well, the rest of the ride's a snap," promised Buddy. "So let's get a move on." He pushed off with his foot, taking the lead once again as we rolled down the road toward home.

"It better be a snap!" Beanie shouted. Turning to me, she said, "You don't think that was a scary ride? Honestly?"

"It was a little scary, Beanie, but it wasn't exactly a *death ride*. Gee whiz. You sure tend to exaggerate."

The rest of the ride *was* a snap. We were back home in ten minutes, greeted by one deliriously happy golden retriever. Beanie went straight into the house, but I stayed back to help Buddy clean up the bikes. It seemed like the right thing to do.

The bikes were kept in a shed in back of the McBeans' main house. I liked the smell of old sheds, and this one was much older than the house itself. I liked the smell of oil and paint, fertilizer and old baseball gloves. Fishing poles, snow skis, shovels and rakes, and large cans of antifreeze and window washing fluid lined the walls and filled all the corners.

We were down on our knees wiping the bikes off when Buddy started asking me questions. Was Kevin Erickson still wrestling? Buddy wanted to know. Did ol' Mr. Hapcheck still chase kids from his lawn with a golf club? Had I heard anything about the winners of the drag races on the Fourth of July, and was Mike Polombo still working three jobs to feed his six kids? I kept sneaking glances at Buddy while I answered his questions as best I could. I still couldn't quite get over it, how different he seemed. It struck me funny, too. To remember how much he'd been a part of my life. And how different I felt about him now.

"What are you smiling about?" asked Buddy a few minutes later.

Embarrassed by my thoughts, I lowered my head.

"Oh, c'mon, just spill it. Can't be that bad."

"The ride we took on your uncle's tractor mower." We'd torn around his aunt and uncle's big yard like a couple of lunatics, then engraved our initials right on the front lawn!

"Oh, that." He laughed when I told him. "Gee, you have a good memory. That was a long time ago. They never paid me, you know. Even after I went back and cut it right."

"Really? They should've paid you!"

He nodded. "They sure should've."

"Do you ever miss it back there?"

He was quiet for a couple of seconds, then he said no, not much. I waited for him to say more, then realized he wasn't going to. At least not about that. There were guys back at home who were easy to talk to, but Buddy wasn't like that. Even as a kid, he kept what he thought to himself. So I didn't ask him the questions I had on my mind. How was high school in California? Had he made new friends? How did he like his job . . . ?

"I hope the ride wasn't too tough for you," he said, looking up from his work a few minutes later. "I guess I didn't pick the easiest trail to start you off on, but it wasn't the toughest, either—not by a long shot."

"Well, that's good, isn't it?" I said. "Otherwise I might have broken my neck."

He sat back on his heels and laughed. "You know, my mom and dad are right. I heard them talking in the kitchen this morning, saying how much you'd changed since we left. I see what they mean. You're really different. You've really grown up."

I felt myself blush, partly with pleasure. So the McBeans had noticed.

"Beanie's thirteen and she seems like . . . Well, she seems like thirteen," he continued. "And sometimes not even *that*, if you know what I mean. But you . . ."

He looked right at me. He was still sitting back on his heels, one hand resting on his knee, the other busy giving Hula a neck rub. She hadn't gotten to go on the ride and now wouldn't let him out of her sight. I blushed again, then scrounged around my mind for something smart to say. "Well, I'm almost fourteen," I informed him, then wished I hadn't. Who cared? It was another stupid remark, and I vowed to keep my mouth shut, which I did—for about seven seconds.

"How do you like your new dog, Buddy?" I asked, reaching over to scratch her head. "She sure seems sweet."

"Oh, she's sweet all right, and gutsy, too. We're a good team, aren't we, girl?"

"I'd forgotten all about Mambo until I saw Hula," I said. "They look so much alike. It's really unbelievable."

He looked up at me in surprise. "Yeah, I guess they do, don't they?"

I felt as if I'd said something wrong and should say I was sorry. But I didn't know what to apologize for.

As he and Hula got into a bit of roughhousing and I went back to dusting the spokes of a bike, I wondered why you'd say something like that about a dog. *And gutsy, too.* It seemed kind of odd. Then I heard those weird words in my head again. *Remember the quarry. Don't forget about the quarry . . .*

"Well, that about does it for this bike," I said, abruptly standing to go. "Beanie's probably wondering what happened to me. I should get in there."

"Oh, I wouldn't worry about Beanie. She's just in there ragging on me to the folks, isn't she, Hula? She's telling them all about the death ride and how lucky she is to be alive!"

I had to smile. Couldn't help it. "Gee, Buddy. I don't think Beanie would say anything to your parents, even if it *was* a death ride."

"It doesn't matter if she does," he said with a certain amount of arrogance, getting to his feet and tossing his rags in the bucket. "They think I'm the greatest. They think I walk on water."

I laughed, just in case I was supposed to. I didn't know what he meant. *Walk on water.* As I watched him hoist one of the bikes onto his shoulder and heave it up onto a wall rack, I realized that whoever or whatever Buddy was or wasn't, he was an unusual guy—and you kind of had to like that.

"Shall we boogie?" he said, turning to me with a smile.

It took me a minute to get what he was saying. That we should go. I thought he was asking me to dance. Dance, there in the shed. I could still be a nutcase at times.

SIX

I AWOKE MONDAY MORNING with stiff legs and a sore butt from our wild bike ride with Buddy, but Beanie woke up with something worse, as I was soon to find out.

I heard her yawn, sigh, and roll over. I was turned toward the wall, reading.

"Madison?" I heard her whisper. "Are you awake?"

"Um-hmm. Been awake for a while. I'm reading."

"What're you reading?"

"*How to Be Happy in High School.*"

"Ugh. I've heard nobody's happy in high school." She yawned.

"I guess that's why somebody wrote the book," I said, turning a page.

"Mmmm . . . Well, then, say the cafeteria at school serves really rotten food. Can the author tell you what to do to fix it?"

"*I* can tell you what to do to fix it. Bring your own lunch."

She laughed. Then she said, "Well, I don't think *I'm* going to be happy in high school."

"Really?" I said with surprise. "How do you know?"

"For one thing, most of the kids I went to school with last year are going to private schools. So I will hardly know anyone."

"But kids always like you, Beanie. You'll make new friends."

"Used to like me. I don't know anymore. Kids in California seem different. And . . ."

"That seems silly, but, yeah, go ahead." Maybe I should have said something right then, just come out and asked her if she was really unhappy. She sure didn't seem much like herself, and I was beginning to wonder if the move to California had been good for everyone except Beanie.

"Well, gee, I never thought I'd be going to high school without you."

She sounded so sad. I lowered my book and sighed. "I know. I never thought it would happen, either. Maybe we can find a way to check out your new school together. Then, when I'm missing you at Glenbard, I can at least picture you somewhere."

"That's a good idea, Maddie. Thanks. I guess I'm just nervous about going."

"I think everyone is. At least, that's what the author says here."

"Really?" she said, sounding happy and relieved. She rolled onto her other side, groaning loudly. I raised my book, hoping to finish the chapter.

"I'm sore all over, aren't you? Darn that Buddy."

I lowered the book. "I'm a little sore, but I'm not sure it's his fault. If it rains, do you blame him for that, too?"

"Very funny."

43

"I'm just teasing. But I've said it before, and I'll say it again: I really don't think he's as bad as he used to be, and I still think you should give him a chance to prove it, instead of assuming he's always out to get you."

"Get real, Maddie. Buddy's been on extra good behavior since you got here. He's just trying to impress you."

"I hardly think so," I replied, rubbing my toes together under the sheets.

"We could've been killed."

"I hardly think that, either." I sighed. "And stop with the melodrama. It's annoying, and not very convincing."

She yawned again. I heard her jaw crack.

"You ought to be careful about all that yawning," I said. I was still facing the wall and still had the book open on the bed in front of me. "Mrs. Perrin's jaw locked shut in the open position, like a pair of steel pliers. She was yawning in church. It was Easter Sunday, and she had to sit in the emergency room for an hour and a half with her mouth stuck open."

"You're joking! You're really kidding me, aren't you?"

"No, it's not a joke. It really happened. It was all over the neighborhood." I felt the start-up of a yawn back in my own throat and immediately began to suppress it, as I had been doing ever since I first heard the story.

"You know, Maddie, things look funny to me this morning. They seem smaller or dimmer or something," murmured Beanie. "It's very, very weird."

"Really?" I replied absently. The book seemed to be geared toward a third-grade reading level. Any second the author was going to say something about waving good-bye to Mommy and Daddy on your first day of school, and I didn't want to miss it.

"I can't even see my feet. Usually, when I look down, I can see my feet poking up from under the blanket, but I can't."

I sighed, put down the book, and rolled over. "Did you check under the bed?"

She was still lying with her head on the pillow. When she turned to look at me, I sucked in my breath, then leaned forward squinting, not sure I was seeing her right. Her eyes were like slits in her face, a face so puffed up and blotchy, it looked like it had been blown up with a bicycle pump. "Be . . . Beanie . . ." I stuttered.

"What? Why are you looking at me like that?"

"It's . . . It's your face, Beanie . . . It's . . ."

She raised a hand to her face, then threw off the covers, scrambled out of bed, and dashed across the room to her bureau. Glaring at herself in the mirror for about half a second, she shrieked, then covered her face with her hands.

"Okay, Beanie, calm down," I said, throwing my legs over the side of the bed and grabbing my sweatpants from a little heap of clothes on the floor. "I'll go get your mother."

"Hurry!" She made a dash for her bed and slid back under the covers. "I knew something was wrong!" she wailed in a muffled voice from under the sheets.

"I am hurrying," I said, stepping into my sweatpants and pulling them up as fast as I could. "Do you have a toothache?"

"No!" she shrieked. "Why should I have a toothache?!"

"My father's face blew up like that once. He had an

45

abscessed tooth. I was only six, and he came into the kitchen in the morning with this monster face and scared the living daylights out of me."

She burst into tears.

I ran downstairs to get her mother.

It was poison oak and not a pretty sight. I went along with Beanie and her mother to see Dr. Tong in some small town close by later that morning, by which time the poison oak had become an ugly red rash bent on overtaking most of Beanie's body. It was grotesque, really ugly stuff, and it creeped me out. The doctor said she must've landed right in the middle of a big patch of the stuff and prescribed two kinds of medicine: a bottle of pills and a sticky white cream to spread all over the rash itself.

"Darn that Buddy, darn that Buddy." Beanie said it whenever we were out of her mother's earshot. If I heard it once, I heard it seventy times. The thing is, she could've said the same thing about me. I'd talked her into going, after all, but I think she preferred blaming Buddy. I didn't think it was really his fault. After all, neither he nor I had ended up in the bushes, and Beanie *was* a bit clumsy. But I did think it was cool of her not to be snitching. On the ride into town, her mom had asked Beanie how come she was the only one who got poison oak when we'd all been on the same ride.

"Fell off my bike," replied Beanie.

"I thought you knew this whole area is loaded with poison oak," said Marie.

I was in the backseat. I couldn't see Marie's face, but she sounded annoyed.

"Weren't you following Buddy the whole way?"

I was a little surprised by her mother's reaction. I'd expected a little more sympathy, but I supposed it was how most parents react in that sort of situation. Certain phrases fly out of their mouths without any aforethought: *Why weren't you more careful? Why didn't you watch where you were going? Next time think before you try something like that.* I figured they said those things to reassure themselves more than anything. And with Beanie looking like she did, maybe her mom needed lots of reassurance. I could've used some, too. I felt bad for Beanie, but I had concerns of my own. How long did it take to get rid of poison oak, and what would this do to my vacation?

"I didn't *plan* on falling, Mother. I didn't get to pick out a good spot. It just so happened I landed in the wrong spot, and I'm sorry it's such an inconvenience. I'm sorry I'm such a klutz and I'm sorry I'm not more like Buddy!"

I thought she was going to cry. I leaned forward and slipped my right hand onto her right shoulder.

"Beanie," her mother said firmly, "that's not what I meant."

"Beanie," I said, keeping my hand on her shoulder. "It wasn't your fault at all. It could've been me just as easily. You must've hit a rut in the road or something."

Beanie didn't say anything. I had a feeling she didn't want me to say more, either, so I kept my trap shut. Instead, I turned and looked out the window at the wind sweeping across the brown grasslands. No, I heard myself think. No, she hadn't hit a rut in the road. We were going too fast and the road was too steep. And, yes, we had followed Buddy every step of the way.

Looking as she did, you couldn't blame Beanie for hiding out in her room. Hula took one look at her and ran. Poor Beanie. It took quite awhile for Marie and me to finally coax her into joining us in the living room. Then, just as she was descending the stairs in her bathrobe—her distorted, tomatolike face bathed in the gunky white cream—who should return home but Buddy?

He strolled into the living room in a pair of cutoffs, a T-shirt, and hiking boots. "Hi, Maddie," he said with a gorgeous smile.

I managed a quick "Hi!" back, but it tumbled out of my mouth so awkwardly and abruptly, it sounded more like something you'd deliver with a karate chop.

Then he saw Beanie.

"Oh, wow. What happened to you, Pizza Face?!"

"You dirty dog!" shouted Beanie from the top of the stairs. She yanked off a thong and hurled it at Buddy. It missed him, landing a few feet from Hula, who fled into the next room with her head and tail hanging.

"I guess that was meant for me," he said wryly, turning toward me.

I shrugged and looked at the floor, not wanting to get caught in the middle again.

"Oh, Buddy," chortled Marie from the kitchen. "You be nice to your sister or else. She's got poison oak, and she's not feeling too good."

"Poison oak?"

He looked at me.

I nodded.

"Uh-oh. Hey, Hula," he called. "I bet I'm the one in trouble, not you!"

It was Buddy's idea to run into town for videos and a pizza. I thought this was nice of him, and it further reinforced my belief that he'd truly changed. I was even more surprised, and flattered and excited, when he invited me to come along. Just the same, I felt nervous getting into a car alone with him a short time later. It wasn't like being in the shed, when I could leave anytime I wanted. What would we talk about, and would I have anything interesting to say?

We rolled down the long dirt driveway in his mother's old Saab with the car in neutral. Then, when we hit the main road, he shifted into first and gunned the engine. Gripping the door handle with my right hand, I asked him how long he'd been driving.

"I got my license last Friday. This is my first time out by myself."

"Oh." I swallowed—you could hear it above the roar of the engine.

He laughed and told me he was kidding. He'd had his license since March and promised not to do anything stupid.

"I wasn't really worrying," I protested. I felt him turn and smile. "But could you keep your eyes on the road?"

He laughed again. I took a deep breath, let go of the door handle, and settled back into the seat. It wasn't so hard thinking of things to say, and soon we were talking about Beanie.

"She's a mess, isn't she?" said Buddy.

"You mean the poison oak?" I asked.

"I mean in general. But it's a good example."

"Hmmm . . ."

"She's afraid of everything, Maddie. Of trying new things, of taking chances, of going too fast on her bike! You know why you and I didn't end up in the bushes like Beanie? Because we weren't afraid of crashing in the first place."

I liked seeing myself through Buddy's eyes, as somebody who wasn't afraid to take chances.

"She does seem a little unsure of herself," I murmured, remembering our talk early that morning. But I felt guilty saying it, like I was talking behind her back, a traitor conspiring with the enemy.

"A *little?* Fear runs her life. It's why I've got to toughen her up, teach her to overcome it."

"Oh, I see, it's Sergeant Buddy McBean."

He laughed, nudging my arm with his elbow.

I jumped a foot.

"You're a crack-up," he said. "That was funny. You know what I mean, though?"

"I don't know. I think we're all different. And I think we're all afraid of *something*, don't you? I think it's sort of . . . normal."

"You think Beanie is normal? You're scaring me, Madison Chimes."

"And you're teasing me, Buddy McBean. I think you know what I'm saying."

He was taking the hairpin turns on the road pretty fast, but I didn't say anything. I didn't want to ruin his image of me as sort of a fearless person, and I didn't want to give into my own fear. So, just when I was sure the car would sail over the side of the road and that would be it, I closed my eyes, gritted my teeth, and said a quick prayer. But nothing like that happened. Maybe Buddy was right.

We ran into a couple of Buddy's friends, Ivan and Augie, at the video place. They seemed like nice guys, and because your friends reveal a lot about you, I scored it as another point in Buddy's favor. I didn't think of this as taking sides. I was just rooting for him to turn out to be a good guy. Maybe I liked him a little bit, too—and if he did turn out to be a nice guy after all, why the heck shouldn't I?

After Buddy introduced me to Ivan and Augie, the three of them started horsing around like guys tend to do. So, feeling a little left out, I walked over to a rack of videos a few feet away, cleverly planting myself within earshot. That was the first time I heard mention of a place called Sculptured Beach, and it was the first time I ever heard anyone dead or alive refer to me as a "babe." I think it was Augie who said it, and maybe I was meant to hear it. I was a "babe" all right. And someday I'd ski down Mount Everest. Become president of Russia.

"Ask her! *Ask her!*" urged Ivan in a hoarse, roaring whisper. He punched Buddy on the shoulder. Buddy walloped him back. We left soon after that. Ask me what? I wondered.

On our way to pick up the pizza, Buddy told me that both Ivan and Augie said I was cute.

"Oh, how sweet," I said, gazing out the side window. I felt a yawn coming on. I sometimes yawned when I was nervous.

"You know, Madison . . ."

He kept turning his head to look at me. I turned away,

to look out the window on my side. "I'm so hungry," I said.

"... I don't think you've exactly caught up with yourself, if you know what I mean."

I slunk way down in my seat, blushing to the roots of my hair. No, I didn't really know what he meant, and I wasn't sure I wanted to. All I saw was a funny picture of myself split in two, one half running ahead and another shadowy self hurrying to keep up.

"Madison?"

"Yeah?" Goose bumps bloomed on my bare arms and legs. I was afraid he was going to *ask me*. I drew my arms in close to my body, sort of hugging myself to keep warm.

"What kind of pizza do you like?"

"What? Oh. I like everything. Just skip the anchovies."

"No little fishies on yours."

I shivered again.

"Cold?"

I nodded. He rolled up his window.

That big yawn was still coming on. I tried everything I could to suppress it, finally covering my mouth with my hand, but it had a mind of its own. "... ahhhhhhhhhhhh ..."

"Hey, sorry I've bored you."

I knew that he knew that I hadn't been bored at all. I knew that he knew that I was kind of thrilled to go for a ride with an older guy, even if it was my best friend's brother. I told him it had been a long day, and I was a little bit tired. He said I was also a little bit shy, just like I'd always been, and he was glad to see I hadn't changed altogether. He said he liked shy people, though, he thought they were interesting.

I looked down at the video in my lap. *Night of the Seventh Nightmare.* Didn't Beanie hate scary movies?

Beanie did. It was kind of pathetic. Here she was, going into high school, and still burying her head under a pillow during the scary parts, though I could hardly blame her on this particular occasion. Who wanted to watch a monster movie when that's what you saw when you looked in the mirror?

I had a hard time falling asleep that night. Ask me what? I kept wondering.

When I did fall asleep, I dreamed about Mambo. That beautiful dog was walking toward me across a still, blue pond. I watched her from a little rowboat out in the middle of the water. As soon as she was close enough for me to reach out and touch, she suddenly began to disappear, slowly slipping beneath the surface of the water. And I felt my heart sinking with her.

When I woke up the next morning, I remembered the dream, and I remembered the story in the Bible about Jesus walking on water. It was a miracle, and it meant He was like God. He could do anything.

They think I walk on water, Buddy had said about his parents. I hoped he wasn't saying what I thought he was saying. It didn't seem right to worship your own kid.

SEVEN

THAT DREAM LEFT ME FEELING a bit blue. I thought maybe I would mention it to Beanie, since telling somebody else about a bad dream usually made me feel better. But when I turned over in bed that morning, I saw that Beanie was already up and gone.

I got myself up, went to the window, and pulled back the curtain, half hoping for rain or fog. I knew we'd had plans to hang out at somebody's pool that day, and I also knew we wouldn't be going. If the weather was at least partly to blame, I might not feel so bad. No such luck, though. The sun was out and not a shred of fog in sight anywhere.

I was about to climb back into bed with my *Seventeen* magazine, then quickly changed my mind. Looking at all those pictures of kids having a great time at the beach would only bum me out more.

I threw on a T-shirt and a pair of jeans and headed downstairs instead. On my way through the living room, I noticed the Scrabble board already set up on the big coffee table in front of the sofa. I sighed.

"How's the poison oak?" I called from the kitchen, trying for a tone of voice that wouldn't betray how I really felt.

"About two percent better." I heard her flip the page of a magazine.

"Out of a hundred?"

"Yep."

I grunted, then grabbed a cereal bowl from the cabinet, filled it half full with granola, and headed back into the living room, where I plopped down onto the floor beside Hula.

It didn't seem fair to be beating Beanie at Scrabble, not with her eyes still so puffy and with the rashes on her face, neck, and legs beginning to ooze. I was glad the medicine had helped with the itching, though it looked an awful lot like Elmer's glue. Poor Beanie.

"*Goad* is not a word," she declared, frowning in concentration down at the board. "I challenge you."

"I accept. Go ahead, look it up if you want." We were sitting on the floor on either side of the coffee table. My legs were still a bit sore from the bike ride, and I gingerly rearranged them underneath the table.

"*Goad* means 'to prod,' like with a stick," I informed her.

Her scowl deepened. I knew she wouldn't challenge me and risk losing her turn. We both knew it. I wondered if Buddy was right. Maybe she was too cautious for her own darn good.

"Look it up or take your turn," I said flatly. It was hard keeping up my enthusiasm for the game. I knew the doctor wanted her to stay out of the sun as much as possible, since sweat tended to make poison oak spread. Looking like she did, she probably didn't want to go anywhere, anyway. But I did. I wanted to go everywhere, and I hated being indoors on a day with a sky so blue it could break your heart.

"Hold your horses."

"So do something."

"I'm thinking."

"Beanie, you've *been* thinking for about seven minutes. Just take your turn."

"So."

I sighed, resting my chin in the palm of my hand and absently ran my fingers through the soft yellow fur on Hula's neck. I gazed at the letters on my rack. *V, D, L, G, A, S, B. Slav*, I thought. *Salg. Vald. Galt. Basl. Glad.* Beanie might have poison oak, but I was just itching for something to happen, and Scrabble wasn't it. Not by a long shot.

"*Radio*," she announced, finally taking her turn.

"That's good, Beanie. You got thirteen points."

"I'll never catch up. Your turn."

"You might, but not if you give up so early in the game." I studied my letters and scanned the board for a place to play *glad*.

"Your turn," said Beanie, about two seconds later.

My hand twitched in my lap. I felt like reaching across the board and grabbing her neck. Instead I put down my *D* and my *G*, and pulled two new letters from the small burgundy bag.

"*Dog*," said Beanie. "Very clever." Hula lifted her head. "Not you, baby," said Beanie. "Go back to sleep."

"Yeah, but look who's winning."

"I know. I'm not very good."

"I'm sorry. I shouldn't have said that. You're usually a good player." I looked out the window. "It's your turn." I sighed.

"You should take Hula for a walk. It would do you both some good."

"What's that supposed to mean?"

"I'm getting on your nerves."

"No, you're not," I said, but I didn't put much into it.

"Yeah, I can tell."

I turned my head toward the window again. "Where is everyone, anyway? How come the house is so quiet?"

"It's a Tuesday. My mom and dad both work, remember? *Fig.* Double word. Fourteen points. If you're asking about Buddy, I don't know where he is. He's gone all the time, and I know he doesn't work every day. So who knows."

"I wasn't asking about Buddy," I rushed to reply.

"Good, because I'm not into keeping track of him, as you can imagine."

I fiddled with my letters, then lifted my head. "Could we at least turn on the radio or play a CD?"

"Sure." She got up and flicked on the FM radio on her parents' stereo, then fished around for a good station.

"Beanie, do you know if most dogs can swim?"

"Gee, what an odd question. How should I know?"

"It's just that I had a really weird dream about Mambo last night, so I was just wondering. Do you remember if Mambo could swim?"

"No, I really don't know. Anyway, you were there that day. I wasn't. It's your turn again."

"I was where *what* day?" I asked, lifting my head in surprise.

"The day Mambo died," she replied matter-of-factly. "Down at the quarry."

"No, I wasn't. What a weird thing to say." I put down my *L* and my *A*. "*Law.* Double word. Twelve points. Let's keep the game moving."

"You should talk."

"No, *you* should."

"What a weird thing to say," I repeated, after a brief lull in the conversation. "I was not at the quarry that day."

"Yeah, you were. You and Buddy. At least that's what you said when you came running home."

I watched as she rearranged the letters on her rack over and over again, then I couldn't hold back any longer. "I think if I came running home, as you say, from the quarry with Buddy the day Mambo died, it's something I would remember." Under the table, my legs were cramping. I briefly considered raising my knee to give the table a good hard jolt.

"You would think so," said Beanie. "Especially since you and Buddy came home and told us all about it. I guess you've just forgotten, that's all. It happens."

"*It happens, it happens,*" I mimicked.

Beanie looked at me in surprise. I could tell she was hurt, too, but at that moment I really didn't care.

"I doubt I'd forget something like *that*, Beanie. Really."

"Whatever. Anyway, you brought it up. I don't have a need to talk about it." She pulled on her lower lip as she gazed at the board.

Whatever, whatever, I silently sang. I felt kind of crazy inside, suddenly hating everything about her, every little gesture, every little comment. Buddy was right. She was a little wimp, and I was glad she'd moved to California. I wouldn't want to hang around with her in high school, anyway. *I don't have a need to talk about it*? Who talked like that, anyway?

"Your *turn*, Beanie," I fumed. "So what exactly did we supposedly say that day that we supposedly ran home from the quarry?"

"Who?"

"The queen of England! Jeez, Beanie, what's wrong with you today? We were talking about Buddy and me just two seconds ago!"

"Now you're getting on my nerve, Madison," she suddenly shot back. "I don't know why you need to keep talking about this. Go ask Buddy. I'd like to finish this game and do something else."

I jumped up from the floor, my head pounding with fury. "I don't want to do anything else with you!" I shrieked. "You take half an hour to take your turn! You make up half a story and won't finish it! I think I'd remember if I was at the quarry with Buddy!"

"Ask Buddy." She gazed up at me calmly, as though I were a lunatic. I felt like a lunatic.

"I don't have to," I said, glaring down at her with my hands on my hips. "I know where I was and where I wasn't."

She shrugged.

"And one more thing. Somebody doesn't get on your *nerve*, Beanie. You have more than one nerve. So somebody gets on your *nerves*, see? And right now all two million of mine feel jangled. So I'm going to take me and my jangled nerves for a nice long walk, and when I get back, in a half hour or so, maybe you'll have taken your turn, and we can finish up this stupid game." I moved toward the door, quickly, because oddly enough I felt close to tears.

"C'mon, Hula," I called.

I turned to glance at Beanie as I followed Hula out the front door and onto the porch, but I couldn't see her face. She had her head down, and I told myself she was still trying to take her turn. But I don't know. She looked so small and sad and forlorn, sitting there alone at that big coffee table. People have fights, I said to myself as I headed down the front steps and across the yard toward the road. Even friends sometimes have arguments. I hated leaving her like that, though, on a day when she still wasn't feeling too good.

When we reached the main road, Hula went one way and I went the other. "Hula! C'mon!" I called. "Let's go this way."

"*Oof!*" she barked back, stopping and turning to look at me. "*Oof oof!*" No, this way, she seemed to be saying.

"Oh, all right," I muttered, ambling along with my head down. When she saw that I was following, she raced way ahead of me up the road, stopping and turning every so often to make sure I was still there. She seemed to know where she was going and was awfully excited to have me along.

I, on the other hand, dragged along behind her with feet that felt heavy and leaden. How did other people have fights that lasted for days or weeks, even months? I already felt guilty for what I'd said to Beanie six minutes ago, but I also felt angry—and puzzled. I figured her memory must've tricked her, and I shouldn't have blown my top. Why *had* I gotten so mad at her, anyway? It just seemed stupid, until I remembered that weird stuff going on in my head about the quarry, which creeped me out to the max. I was turning into some kind of a head case.

We'd only gone maybe a quarter of a mile when suddenly Hula squirted off into the deep woods lining the side of the road. "Hula!" I shouted. I ran ahead, then tore through the woods still bellowing her name, surprised to discover I was moving along a narrow overgrown trail. Somewhere off in the distance, I could hear Hula barking her head off, and I followed. Not a good idea to go home without her, I thought with a shudder. Oh sure, come to visit the McBeans and lose their dog in the woods. Panic-stricken, I charged ahead, vainly trying to catch up with her. Where was she taking me, and why?

Lucky for me she kept up her yelping. I chased after her for several minutes, crossing a footbridge over a dried-up streambed, following the trail as it zigzagged this way and that, uphill and downhill. I was tired and I was worried. What if the trail had split off without my noticing and I couldn't find my way back?

I dropped to my knees, gulped air, and wiped the sweat from my forehead. "Darn you, Hula," I murmured. I was tired of the game and wanted to go back. Then, when I looked up, I saw I was right in the middle of a redwood grove, the trees so straight and tall they seemed to come together overhead in a single point, like a handful of pencils. An owl hooted and a woodpecker hammered away. Hula had stopped barking. I felt a twinge of fear and excitement in the pit of my stomach. Was I lost? Lost in the woods in California? Would my parents get a call from a sheriff or ranger? Would my friends read about me in the Chicago *Tribune*? Poor me!

"*Oof oof oof!*" Three sharp barks in a row sent me scrambling to my feet and charging up the trail. There she was, wiggling and yelping from a rise in the path ahead of me. Hula, you little devil. C'mon, she seemed to be saying, hurry up! What's taking you so long?

"I'm comin', Hula," I huffed. "I'm comin'." But no sooner did I catch sight of her than I lost her again. Standing in the middle of the trail with my hands on my hips, I peered into the thick woods all around me. This was crazy. "Hula?" I tried. Nothing. Then I noticed a clearing in the woods to my right and a barely noticeable footpath leading to it.

Worth a try, I thought, and took ten or twelve quick steps along this new path, which brought me out into an open clearing. I raised my hand trying to shield my eyes from the sudden shower of sunlight. There was Hula, waiting for me on the front step of an old weather-beaten shack sitting in the middle of the clearing.

"Hula," I said, half under my breath. "What in the world . . . ?" Before I could finish the question, she'd slipped away again, this time through the shack's half-open door, open, perhaps, because it was falling off its hinges and couldn't be shut. I cocked my ear in the direction of a whirring sound, followed by a *tap-tap-tap, tap-tap-tap.*

I felt like Gretl, and the Old Woman soon would show her face in a window or wave a crooked finger at me from the doorway. But this decrepit old place was no gingerbread house—that was for darn sure.

"Doggone you, Hula," I whispered, hugging my arms to my chest to keep from shivering. The place had a funny feel about it, and I preferred not to get closer. But I couldn't turn back without Hula.

As the goose bumps rose on my arms, I crept cautiously

forward across a carpet of stubbly burnt grass. Surely nobody would live in a place like this. The windows were broken and the roof was full of holes. Yet someone seemed to be there, and I was a potential intruder. No gun barrels poking through a window just yet, so I snuck up close to a busted window and peered through it.

I gasped, then quickly pulled my head back, plastering myself against the side of the shack for several long seconds. Somebody *was* in there! My heart began to race wildly, and my feet wanted to do the same. I didn't run, though. I didn't have Hula, for one thing. Instead I inched my face close to the window again, straining to see through the glare of the sun's reflection. I saw a guy with a tool in his hand, kneeling on the floor. Then Hula saw me. *"Oof oof!"* The guy turned. It was Buddy.

Who was more surprised, Buddy or me? For a second or two, he didn't move or say anything, just knelt there gazing blankly at me through the window. Then he slowly rose to his feet, tossing the tool in his hand aside on his way to the door.

"Maddie! What the heck are you doing here?" he asked, stepping through the doorway and onto a single slat of wood that apparently served as a doorstep.

Shock at finding him out here in the middle of nowhere was followed quickly by disappointment. It didn't feel like much of a welcome, and I didn't like to be where I wasn't welcome.

"Hi . . . Hi, Buddy," I blurted, turning away from the window. I squeezed my hands together behind my back, trying to steady my nerves.

"I . . . I just went for a walk with Hula, and she was sort of leading the way. I thought I was lost, but here . . . here I am." I shrugged, but it wasn't an I-don't-care kind of shrug. It was a gee-I'm-sorry-I'm-alive kind of shrug.

He had a peculiar, suspicious sort of look on his face, like he couldn't decide whether or not to believe me and whether or not to invite me in. At that moment, standing on the doorstep, he looked so much like the old Buddy from La Grange, I wanted to turn and run. Then, to my big relief, he seemed to snap out of it.

"So Hula dragged you all the way out here," he said with a small but sweet smile. "Good girl, Hula." Then Hula appeared in the doorway beside him, head held high and tail wagging, proud of her performance.

"Hey, well, c'mon in," said Buddy, motioning me inside with his head.

"I should get back . . ." I started to say, but he'd stepped back inside and was immediately swallowed up by the shadows in the shack.

I hesitated, then stepped away from the window and shuffled through the scrubby grass with a furrowed brow. What was he doing all the way out here in a wreck of a shack in the middle of the woods, and what was I doing out here with him? I still felt like an intruder and must've looked like a wreck myself, all hot and sweaty, and nervous besides. I shouldn't have gone in, but I did because I wanted to. And because he'd asked me to, and at that particular moment on that particular day— which looked to offer little more than some big disappointments—I accepted. When I got to the door, I tripped going through, feeling nearly as unhinged as the door itself.

"Hey, you better watch it," Buddy cautioned. "I don't have insurance, you know, and there are plenty of holes in the floorboards."

Coming right in from the bright sunlight, I could hardly see anything, much less the holes in the floorboards, but I could tell by the sound of his voice I really was welcome. As I made a quick scan of the place, Hula nuzzled up to me and I bent to scratch her forehead. The place was a mess. There were bikes, bicycle parts, and tools all over the place, cans of spray paint, buckets of rags, a small stool. . . .

"I work on bikes, fix 'em up, and sell 'em," explained Buddy.

"Oh, I see," I murmured. "Kind of a hobby of yours."

"Sort of. More like a business than a hobby," he replied, with a wry sort of grin.

I liked the way his gray T-shirt, stained with grease, fit him, the way the muscles in his arms ran like ropes from shoulder to wrist.

He smiled and handed me a plastic container of water.

I took a few gulps and handed it back, our fingers grazing in the exchange. He was studying my face. I looked away.

Hula nuzzled herself against my hip again. "You little trickster," I said, patting her head. "Let's not enroll you as a guide dog for the blind."

"See what a good dog she is. I've been asking her to find me a cute girl for some time now, and she's finally found one, haven't you, girl? Good dog, good dog, Hula."

I blushed down to the roots of my hair, poking my hands deep into the pockets of my cutoffs. I imagined he had a big cocky grin on his face, but I couldn't look at him. If I looked at him, I'd have to think of something to say back, which I suppose would've been better than the dippy look I had on my face, I'm sure. But my brain was on idle.

"I . . . I should get back," I blurted. "I'm right in the middle of a Scrabble game with Beanie."

"Ahh, you don't want to miss *that*, now do you?"

I pressed my lips together to keep them from quivering. No guy had ever made me this nervous before. I didn't like it. I did like it. "I like Scrabble," I said, cringing as soon as the words were out. Bozo, I said to myself.

"Do you? Well I like Yamahas and Suzukis. How about going for a ride?" He said this in the most casual way, like he'd just asked me to go out for ice cream.

"What?"

"I've got a little Yahama. It's nothing fancy. How about a spin down the road?"

He must've seen the look on my face.

"I'll have you back in no time," he added. Then he stood with his hands on his hips, waiting.

"A *motorcycle?*" I said, the bottom falling out of my stomach. Then I saw it. This silver-and-black machine gleaming at me from a corner of the shack.

"Yep, there she is." He threw his head back and guzzled some water, then headed straight for the Yamaha.

"I don't know . . ." All of the things my parents had ever said to me about being careful—I couldn't hear any of them now. I couldn't remember one thing. But I *could feel* them in the muscles and bones of my body holding me back.

"Don't worry! There's a nice little road for riding—it's flat. You'll love it. It'll be fun." He pulled the bike into a full upright position, released the kickstand, and rolled it right out the door. He wasn't giving me much of a chance to say no, and maybe I didn't want to anyway.

I felt myself sort of drift out the door right behind him. In two seconds, I was climbing onto the back of his sleek silver-and-black Yamaha. I knew how to do it, too. Throw a leg over the seat and grab hold of the guy's waist. I'd seen it in movies. Inside, I was scared but smiling. It would be a great story to tell back home . . .

He kick-started the engine, and the Yamaha began to rumble and shake underneath me.

"Hey, Maddie!" He was hollering above the whir of the engine.

"Yeah?" I leaned forward, cocking my head to one side.

"I'd appreciate it if you didn't mention this place to any-body else. It's a private thing. And don't say anything about the Yamaha, either. Okay?"

"Sure." I nodded my head, forgetting he couldn't even see me.

Then he shifted into gear, and away we went, my hair swirling about my head and face like the mane of a wild pony as we roared across the meadow.

I could see why people did this. You left every care you ever had in the dust.

We soon left the meadow behind, tearing through the woods on a flat dusty fire road. I could hardly believe it was me. And what would I be doing at home on a Tuesday after-noon in August? Mowing the lawn? Reading on a wicker chair in the yard? Baby-sitting my sister at the pool mobbed with screaming children? Get a look at me in California!

I clung to Buddy's waist and gripped the bike with my knees. Then, over Buddy's shoulder, I saw a creek a little way ahead, but no way to get across it. Not until we got closer, and I saw a long narrow plank of wood spanning the width of the creek. We were heading right toward it.

"Buddy!" I hollered.

"What?" he hollered back, half turning.

"We're not going to cr . . . ?" My throat closed up around the rest of my sentence like a little trap door. I could see he wasn't stopping. So I hung on tight and said a quick prayer. Suddenly we were rumbling across that skinny wooden plank—*bam bam bam bam*. I gritted my teeth and cringed. We were several feet above a dry, rocky creek bed, and I was sure if I leaned just a little to one side or the other, we'd flip and go over, following my stomach to the bottom of the gulch.

Bam bam bam bam. My insides felt like they wouldn't hold together. Then, suddenly we were over, the road on the other side of the creek dropping away so that, instead of immediately hitting ground, we were airborne for several seconds. We were flying, and I was super-alive!

EIGHT

I DIDN'T NOTICE THE BLOOD seeping through my pants leg until I was halfway home. Standing beneath those same pretty redwood trees, I pulled the pants leg up past my knee and gasped. My left knee was bloody and studded with cinders. Up until then, I'd figured it was just a bit banged up from the fall.

What happened wasn't Buddy's fault—or mine, either, for that matter. The bike had simply hit a rock or a bump in the road as it came down after soaring across the "bridge," careening out from underneath us. I had scrapes on my hands and elbows, but my poor left leg had obviously gotten the worst of it. Buddy had a few scrapes on his hands like me, but that was it. Maybe having the handlebars to hang on to had saved him.

Limping as I was, it took me twice as long to get back to the McBeans' place as it had to get to the woods. I didn't mind, though. I didn't even mind the pain. I was still super-high from the ride itself. Every time I went over what happened, how we zoomed from bank to bank over the creek on a couple of rickety boards, I got the same sharp dig in the pit of my stomach. We could've gone right over the side! I could've shifted my weight a little to the left or a little to the right and bingo! Or the boards could've flipped! I could be dead by now, or paralyzed from the waist down!

I kept seeing how it could have happened, me and Buddy and the Yamaha hurtling into the rocky ravine. I shuddered from the thrill of it all and blinked my eyes. I'd do it again. That's what I would tell Buddy when I saw him. I'd do it again in a second, I would!

By the time I got home, the Scrabble game was gone, and so was Beanie. After I hobbled up the stairs and down the hall into the bathroom, I shut the door, then stood there for a couple of seconds, hands at my side in front of the sink. My mother would know what to do to fix my leg, but I wasn't sure that I did. I felt kind of lost and a little sorry for myself, but then I snapped out of it and took charge. I had to. My mother was not here, and I was. Then I began to search the bathroom cabinets for stuff I might need—a small pair of tweezers, a bottle of hydrogen peroxide, a bag of cotton balls, and some Band-Aids and gauze.

I bit down on my lower lip as I ran hot water from the bathtub faucet onto my leg and clenched my teeth as I dumped a few capfuls of the peroxide right into the part that was all shredded up. Then I started extracting the cinders one by one with the little tweezers, knowing Buddy would be proud of me for not howling from the pain, as I easily could have.

He'd been so sweet after our crash, helping me up off the ground, checking me over for broken bones, pouring water on my scraped-up elbows. Then, as though I'd just passed some sort of major test, he'd come right out and *asked me.*

Did I want to go to this thing at Sculptured Beach on Saturday? Yeah! Sure! I wanted to blurt, without even thinking. But I asked him what thing on Saturday. I did this on behalf of my parents, who would've asked the same question and more.

I extracted another cinder, setting it atop the growing pile along the ledge of the bathtub, and winced as I dabbed at the open cuts with a cotton ball soaked in peroxide.

Just some friends going to the beach, said Buddy. It was a great beach, and it was no big deal or anything, but maybe I'd want to come along. Ivan and Augie would be there, and others.

I saw it all in my mind, just like the pictures in *Seventeen* magazine. Ten kids eating hot dogs on top of a Volkswagen. A bunch of kids making pyramids in the sand. Of course I wanted to go, but I didn't know what to do about Beanie. I didn't want to leave her behind, and I was embarrassed to come right out and say so.

I told Buddy I had to see.

"See what?" he'd said. "Into your crystal ball?"

He was quick with the one-liners. I couldn't keep up.

I guessed he knew what I meant all along, because the next thing he said was it was okay to bring Beanie, and a small price to pay. I felt split down the middle. Happy for me, because he really seemed to want me to go. Unhappy for Beanie, who, for all he seemed to care, could've been a fruitfly.

With the tweezers poised in midair and my left foot resting on the pale blue ledge of the tub, I stopped what I was doing to wonder about Beanie. I was really sorry about our fight and sorry I'd gotten so bent out of shape about nothing. Who cared about something that happened so long ago, anyway? But I knew I was right, and now I wished I'd asked Buddy about the quarry while I had the chance. Then I'd be able to tell Beanie that no, he didn't remember me being with him at the quarry, either, and that would be it, period, end of discussion.

I turned and stood up straight, glancing at myself in the mirror above the sink, at the small scrape on my chin. How would I explain *that* to the McBeans without breaking my promise to Buddy? I'd turn it into a joke, that was how. I wouldn't have to lie. I would just say I was in competition with Beanie for facial abnormalities.

Part of me didn't care if they found out, anyway, if they fussed a bit over me or told me to be more careful. I not only wanted them to think me funny and smart, I wanted them to think me a bit reckless, too, and foolhardy. A bit like Buddy. Whom they adored.

I hid the bloody cotton balls in the bottom of the wastebasket, swept the little pile of cinders and empty Band-Aid wrappers into the palm of my hand, then dumped them into the toilet and flushed. Life was so funny! I thought, as I pulled on a pair of loose-fitting sweatpants and tied the drawstring in a bow around my waist. Here I was all banged up and in pain, digging cinders from my leg, and I'd never been happier.

I snuck in a last glimpse of myself in the mirror, tucking my straight shoulder-length hair behind my ears. (Maybe Buddy was right. Maybe I did look older than my age.) Then I limped my way down the hallway and stairs to go hunt for Beanie.

I found her reading in a hammock in a shady spot out back of the house. "Hey," I called to her, "wait till you see what a klutzy fool I've been!"

We got along better after that. My "battle scars" seemed to even things out between us, but I didn't show her my leg. I didn't think I could fool her into thinking that could've happened simply from a fall in the woods.

Later that night, up in Beanie's room, I asked her if Buddy had a girlfriend. She was working on a watercolor, copying a picture of a pretty seascape out of a book.

She lifted her head and gave me an incredulous look. "Buddy? You've got to be kidding." She snickered in such a way as to make the idea only a remote possibility.

"Well, he is sixteen now," I said with some gusto. "Guys that age do look at girls. And he's not bad looking." (Not *bad?* I laughed to myself. There's an understatement if I ever heard one!)

"I hadn't noticed."

"Guess it's time to take another look, isn't it?"

"Why should I? He's still a jerk."

"*I* hadn't noticed."

We didn't talk for a while. I watched her paint and gazed out the window, wondering how I should ask the next question.

"Beanie," I began after some time, "your brother's invited us to some sort of a thing at a place called Sculptured Beach on Saturday. It sounds like fun to me. You want to go?" I held my breath, waiting.

"What do you think?" she said sarcastically, lifting her head. I looked thoughtfully at the ugly red rashes on her face, neck, and arms, wondering if maybe she *was* still mad at me. "Your rashes are definitely fading," I declared. "I think they'll be totally gone by Saturday." I tried my best to sound certain, even though what I was saying was an incredible stretch of the truth.

"Well, rashes or not, I'm not sure I want to go anywhere with Buddy. Why should I? He makes my life so miserable." She dipped a long-handled paintbrush into a small vat of red paint and waved it across a damp sheet of paper.

"Oh, Beanie." I sighed.

"'Oh, Beanie' what? You know how he is. You know how mean he's always been. He can't just let me alone. Now that he's older, he thinks he can change me or something. He thinks if he pushes a little harder, he can turn me into a cliff diver or a world-class surfing dude."

I had to laugh. I just couldn't help it, and I couldn't help noticing how good a painter she'd become, either.

"You're good, Beanie. Have you been taking lessons?"

"No. Just classes at school. I can't really paint. I'm not good at anything."

"Stop talking like that. I hate it. You're good at a lot of things. I was even wondering why your parents don't hang any of your paintings. They're so into art, and your stuff is so good."

"They're *into* Chagall."

"*Who?*"

"A French painter. Never mind. I don't really expect them to hang my stuff next to his."

I thought about some of the truly awful stuff "created" by my sister and me, stuff my parents had proudly plastered the walls with down through the years. It must've frightened people who came to visit but my parents did it, anyway. I supposed you couldn't expect Dennis and Marie to do the same thing, since they were art *collectors*, and their tastes were so much more refined. Still, if it were *my* kid . . .

"Beanie, I'd love something of yours to take home with me. If you have something you don't mind giving away, I'd put it up in my room."

She looked up at me in surprise. "You're kidding, right?"

"Course not. I'd love something you've done. I really, really would."

She lowered her head, but not before I saw her lower lip begin to quiver. I leaned closer, feeling as though the time had come to find out what was really going on.

"Beanie, what's wrong?"

"I know you're being nice to me. You always have been. But I'm really not good at anything. I never have been. It's just who I am." Tears slid from her cheeks, dropping into the swirl of color on the paper.

I felt my face get hot, but not from embarrassment. It was anger boiling up inside me, but I wasn't sure who to be mad at.

"Why would you cut yourself down like that, Beanie? What you're saying isn't true. You're a wonderful person, kind and smart and sweet. Everybody has always liked you, but if you keep feeling like *that*, you're going to run into trouble."

She lifted her head and looked at me with her big sad eyes. "I don't feel like a wonderful person."

"Well, you are. And you shouldn't let your brother get to

you. Don't take it to heart, and he'll probably leave you alone."

"He's always left me alone," she murmured. "In a way."

She seemed so lonely and sad, I felt like crying right with her.

"And we don't have to go on Saturday," I added. "It's not worth it if you're not going to have a good time, and I won't go without you. We can do something else. It's not that important."

"It's hard to know what to do," she moaned. "I don't want to ruin your vacation, but I really don't want to hang out with Buddy, either."

"You're not ruining my vacation at all. I'm having a great time." I swallowed hard, knowing I'd probably let go of a big day at the beach.

Beanie put down her paintbrush and looked me square in the eye. "I can always count on you to tell me the truth, can't I, Maddie? It's really been hard not having you around. I'll tell you what. If my rash clears, I'll at least think about going."

That's how unselfish Beanie was and why she was such a good friend.

She seemed to feel better after our talk. Sitting on the floor between the two beds, laughing and chattering our heads off, we each polished off a huge bowl of rocky road ice cream. It was a blast, exactly like the old times back in La Grange. Just the two of us. I decided right then I'd put all my effort and time into being with Beanie from that moment on. I'd forget about boys and stuff my *Seventeen* magazine back into my duffel bag. Just making my mind up made me feel closer to Beanie.

Except that my poor leg was killing me, and every time I tried to move it or bend it, I saw a vision of myself sailing over the creek on the Yamaha. I didn't say anything to Beanie, of course, because I'd promised not to. I only half wanted to tell her, anyway. The other half of me liked keeping it to myself, like a bag of candy you keep hidden in the bottom of your drawer.

These ironic things also kept popping into my mind. That I *had* really gone on a "death ride." That we were eating rocky road ice cream, and I'd just dug a pile of cinders from my leg. Still, when we went to bed later that night, I felt closer to Beanie than I had the whole trip. I was worried about her, too, and lay awake wondering if her parents knew how unhappy and unsure of herself she seemed to be here in California. If they did, I hadn't seen any sign of it.

I was nearly asleep when a car door slammed shut just outside the house, jerking me back to a wide-awake state. Then I heard someone walking alongside the house. I figured it was Buddy coming home from work and got up to peek.

Beanie's room was situated at the very end of the second-floor hallway. A large window overlooked the deck out back, but from a small side window you could see the area at the right side of the house.

It was Buddy, and he looked gorgeous, like some kind of god striding across the moonlit yard. His white shirt seemed to glow in the dark. I should've jumped back behind the curtain right then, because he was headed toward the side door right underneath my window, but for some reason I didn't. I stood there looking. Just as I was about to step back from the window, he raised his head and looked right at me. I froze. He stopped dead in his tracks, head lifted, feet planted slightly apart.

You hear people say that time stood still. That always sounded corny to me, but that was exactly what happened. I didn't move; I didn't breathe. I don't know how long we stood there like that, maybe just a few seconds—too long, and not long enough.

My face on fire, my heart thumping wildly in my chest, I jumped backward, then dove for my bed. It's only Buddy, I said to myself, grabbing the covers and pulling them over my head. It's only Buddy. It's only Buddy. But who was I kidding?

Remember the quarry, said the voice in my head. It was like one part of me talking to another part of me from a different room in my mind. I was really starting to wonder about all that quarry stuff, and when my eyes finally began to close that night and I began to drop down into sleep, I suddenly felt as if I couldn't breathe, as if I were half under water.

If this was "falling in love," I wasn't sure I was going to like it.

NINE

THE DOOR TO BUDDY'S ROOM was closed when we left the next morning. I didn't know if he was in there or not, but I was glad to get out of the house before I had to see him, not yet having decided whether or not I'd made a fool of myself standing at the window last night. Who did I think we were—Romeo and Juliet? And if I hadn't made a fool of myself, if what I thought was happening really was happening, well . . . Let's say no guy had ever looked at me like that before. And my idea to forget about boys suddenly made no sense at all.

On her way to work, Beanie's mother dropped me and Beanie off on Main Street in Point Reyes Station. We wandered around town for a while, checking out the shops and doing some exploring. Maybe I wasn't ready to face Buddy alone, but I kept hoping we'd run into him. When I heard the roar of a motorcycle down Main Street, I felt all tingly inside and quickly raised my head, disappointed to see some guy with a long red beard fly by us.

We had lunch with Beanie's friend Tina and Tina's mother at the Station House Café, then zipped up to Santa Rosa to go to the movies. Beanie wore her sunglasses because her eyes were still puffy and kept them on during the movie.

"What just happened? Why did she say that?" Beanie kept asking me. "Who's that guy in the red T-shirt?" I told her to take off her glasses and stop driving me nuts. Tina's mother finally leaned forward and gave her a look, and that shushed her up.

But it was not only Beanie bothering me. I was driving myself nuts, too, wondering if I should just forget about going to the beach with Buddy. I wanted to do the right thing for Beanie. I really did. But I also seemed to want what I wanted. I didn't realize I was biting my nails—*crunch crunch crunch*—until Tina's mother, two seats away, leaned forward to give me a look, too. I stopped.

Would I go without Beanie? I knew what my parents would say. But they weren't here, were they? And what they didn't know wouldn't hurt them. I was almost fourteen, and you had to start living your own life sometime.

The movie itself was silly. I had a better time with the pictures in my mind, like flying across the meadow on Buddy's Yamaha. But when the girl star kissed the boy star, I felt that kiss down to my toes.

I wondered if Beanie was wrong about Buddy. He could have a girlfriend. He could have two or three, for that matter, without anyone knowing, and the longer I sat there wondering and thinking about it, the more I was sure it was true. Nicole? Kelley? Stacey? Did she look like this doll in the movie?

On our way out of the theater, Beanie tripped and went sprawling down the center of the aisle. I heard a commotion and turned. She was down on her hands and knees on the floor behind me, her sunglasses resting precariously on the tip of her nose. Malt balls squirted down the aisle like marbles.

I let out a snort, then covered my mouth when I saw the look on Tina's mom's face. I reached out to Beanie to give her my hand, but it was still slick from the buttered popcorn, and she slid back down to the floor. We started to laugh and couldn't stop, and soon a sort of hysteria set in. Limp and exhausted from laughing, we ended up in a heap on the floor in the center aisle, "a serious fire hazard," as some grumpy person noted. Tina's mother, smiling stiffly, pulled us each to our feet.

Once more it was like the old days, when having a best friend was the only thing that mattered, and in a way I hoped and wished it could be the same forever. But deep down, I knew I was changing. I knew there was more out there, and I had to know what it was.

Buddy worked the evening shift, so I didn't see him at all that day. It was the end of my fifth full day in California. I had eight days left, and they were going by fast.

Thursday was Girls Day Out. Marie was taking the day off work to take us to San Francisco. Before we left, Beanie said she was going to ask her mother if we could go to the beach party on Saturday.

"Are you sure you want to go?" I asked, holding my breath. I *really* wanted to go, and I *really* didn't want her to go just for me if she was going to be miserable.

"Don't you want me to go?"

"Of course," I said vehemently. "I just don't want you to go if it's going to be awful for you."

"I know I have to change. I need to try things. If it's awful, I'll just hang out with you."

"Good," I mumbled. I was glad she'd decided to go. I thought it would be good for her, and I didn't really want to go alone, but I hoped her plan to hang out with me didn't mean we'd be joined at the hip. "Two peas in a pod" didn't work everywhere.

Marie bought Beanie and me little cable car charms in Chinatown, then took us out for a fabulous Vietnamese lunch and for hot fudge sundaes at Ghirardelli Square. Impressing the McBeans was always a primary goal of mine, but today I had an especially good motive. I hoped my funny comments and witty observations would put Marie in a good mood and keep her there. A "yes" from her would have a huge effect on my immediate future.

Beanie finally popped the question on our way home from the city.

"The beach? On Saturday?" said her mom. "Who's going?"

Beanie turned in her seat. "Who's going?"

"I don't know," I said with reluctance. "I guess Ivan and Augie."

Beanie smiled, then tried to cover it up. I'd ask her why later.

"Well, how would you get there?" asked Marie.

"I . . . I'm not sure." I knew these weren't the right answers and would not incline my own parents toward letting me go.

"I think Buddy might be driving," I hurriedly added.

"Buddy? Why didn't you say so?" said Marie.

Beanie turned to give me a look, rolling her eyes, and I thought about what Buddy had said back in the shed behind the house on Sunday. *They think I walk on water.*

"I'll mention it to your father," said Marie. "But it sounds okay to me."

It sounded like a done deal, and I felt a surge of excitement run through me.

"Cool," said Beanie.

"Great," I added.

When we arrived home early in the evening, Dennis and Buddy were eating spaghetti at the kitchen table. Huge plates of it smothered in a heavy red meat sauce. I was stuffed to my eyeballs and couldn't even look at the stuff, nor at Buddy, suddenly overcome by a fit of shyness.

"Men work hard. Eat spaghetti," said Dennis, lifting his fork.

"Big Chief Dennis," said Marie, setting three big mugs of cinnamon tea on the table. "Make own spaghetti."

"Big Chief Boyardee. He make spaghetti," said Dennis.

"Big Chief Dennis has spaghetti sauce on his nose. Look silly," said Marie.

"War paint," said Dennis, thumping the end of his fork on the table. "Maddie have war paint, too."

He meant the scrape on my chin, which nobody had made too big a deal about. What a relief, not being with a bunch of worriers.

Well, I could just tell. This was going to be one of those nights. We would laugh ourselves silly. But I felt really nervous around Buddy, not having seen him since the incident at the window.

"So Buddy," said Marie, "your sister mentioned something about a party on Saturday. Could you give your father and me a quick rundown."

I gazed self-consciously into my mug of hot tea, knowing Buddy would know I wanted to go.

"Party? What party?" said Buddy.

I looked up in surprise and dismay. Had it been called off, or . . . ?

"I said rundown, not runaround," said Marie, with a wink in my direction.

"Well, it's not really a party," said Buddy. "It's just kind of a *thing*. But what do you want to know? Ask me anything." He lowered his head, inhaling several long strands of spaghetti right from the plate.

Everyone laughed. "Oh, Buddy," murmured Marie, shaking her head.

"Oh, Buddy," my mother would've said. "You are now excused from the table."

"What should we bring?" asked Beanie.

"We?" said Buddy. "Uh-oh."

Beanie's face fell. I felt really bad for her—the last thing she needed was to feel left out. And had I somehow screwed up? Hadn't Buddy said I could ask her?

"Beanie," explained her mother, "he's just kidding."

"Right," muttered Beanie.

"Hey, back up," said Dennis. "Let's start with who's going."

"Yeah, who's going?" said Beanie, a bit meekly this time.

"The usual," said Buddy, wiping his mouth with the back of his hand.

"The usual," repeated his father. "Buddy, you ought to consider a career with the CIA. Getting information from you has never been easy. I want details, and I want them now, or some of this spaghetti is going to end up wrapped around your neck."

"You want a guest list? Printed on nice stationery?"

"Buddy. Answer your father's question."

"Okay," said Buddy, dipping his head to inhale more spaghetti.

I looked away, half amused and half repulsed. "IvanAugieDerkMindyTimBrianRandiJasonBethKimChico TomDickandHarry."

We cracked up again. It was brilliant.

"I know Ivan," said Marie. "He seems like a nice kid."

I glanced at Beanie, who was blushing. Aha again.

"The others are nice kids, too?" asked Dennis.

"Not really," replied Buddy. "Most of them just got out of prison."

I bit my lip to keep from snorting.

"Isn't he something?" said Dennis to me. "What a character. A straight answer would be nice, Buddy. Otherwise . . ."

"Otherwise nobody'll be going anywhere. I know. Yeah, the others are cool, just like me. Hey, I just thought this would be a fun thing for Madison, a real California kind of thing, you know?"

Dennis and Marie both nodded. I gazed into my cup, waiting.

"Wouldn't it be fun for me, too?" asked Beanie.

I cringed, because I knew she was setting herself up, a sitting duck for another zinger from Buddy.

"Sure. I'll put you in a little tub and push you out to sea. Then we'll all be happy," cracked Buddy.

"Thanks a lot, Buddy. I love you, too."

Buddy's teasing was hurting her feelings. I could see it, and I thought Dennis and Marie could see it, too. I waited for them to do something, afraid Beanie might end up in tears right here at the table.

"Beanie," said Dennis, "Buddy's just teasing. Don't be so sensitive."

I swallowed, disappointed in her father's response. I looked at Marie, waiting for her to say more.

"Rub-a-dub-dub," said Buddy, grinning in my direction. I pressed my lips together and looked away. Enough was enough. Somebody should stop him.

"Okay, Buddy," sighed Marie without much gusto. "Stop teasing your sister."

"Sorry," said Buddy. "Just having some fun." But he didn't look sorry.

"Okay, wise guy," said Dennis. "Button it up, and you take good care of these two."

The thing at the beach. We were going! I'd almost forgotten the point of the conversation.

"That's okay," said Beanie. "I don't think I want to go, anyway."

I gave her a swift kick under the table. It was probably selfish, but I still wanted to go.

"Oh, c'mon," said Buddy. "I was just having some fun."

Beanie was no dummy. I figured she knew Buddy

wouldn't have asked her to go if it wasn't for me. She still looked surprised, though. I saw a flicker of hope, too, quicker than the blink of an eye, that maybe her brother really wanted her to come.

"Oh, okay, I'll go," she mumbled.

"All right then," said Dennis. "Now, we don't want them going in the water. It's too unpredictable out there, and I don't want to spend the day worrying. And we want them home by dark."

"No problem," said Buddy. He looked at me and smiled, slouched way back in his chair.

I couldn't help smiling, then grabbed the newspaper off the table, pretending to read, shielding my face from Buddy. I didn't want him to see how happy I was that we were going.

The *Point Reyes Light* was a small local paper, about twenty pages in all. "This paper is so cute," I said, flipping through it.

"So are you," said Buddy.

"You're such a jerk," said Beanie.

"Hey, like shoot me."

"Hey, like don't tempt me."

"Buddy!" tittered Marie. "Stop flirting with your sister's best friend."

My face burned behind the paper. Beanie kicked me under the table and I kicked her back.

"Takes after his old man," said Dennis.

"Oh, you think so," said Marie.

"Oh, to be sixteen," said Dennis.

"Oh, to be twenty," said Buddy.

It sounded as if everybody was laughing but me. I made laughing sounds but they were fakes. I was too embarrassed to really laugh.

"What's the joke? I don't get it," said Beanie.

I peered at her over the top of the newspaper. Ah, somebody else who wasn't laughing.

"We're just fooling around," said Marie. "Just having some fun."

"You wouldn't understand," said Buddy.

"I'm not stupid," muttered Beanie.

"Could've fooled me."

They were at it again.

"That's enough," said Dennis.

I heartily agreed. Enough was enough. I didn't want any more trouble. I didn't want to be disappointed in people I liked. I just wanted to laugh and be happy.

"Wow, look at this," I exclaimed. "Here's a column listing all the weekly calls to the local police departments."

"Oh, those are a crack-up," said Marie. "Like somebody picked some peonies from so-and-so's garden without asking."

"Or so-and-so was missing a wheelbarrow but later found it in his own basement," said Dennis. He got up to clear the dishes from the table. "Read some. We need a good laugh."

"Out loud?" I asked.

"Yeah."

For a second I longed for the old days, when I wasn't so darn self-conscious in front of Buddy, but I cleared my throat and began to read.

"'A thief stole two *fishing poles* from a man's boat on Alpine Lake.'"

"'The fire department found a set of *keys* on Waller Road.'" I lifted my head. "Isn't that just awful?"

"Awful," murmured a chorus of McBeans.

"Here's another. 'A man reported hearing a car skid to a stop in front of his house and then roar off.'"

"That's terrible. I hope they've caught the guy by now," said Beanie.

"'A cat set off a burglar alarm in the Inverness Post Office.'"

"I'm not making these up," I said. "Honest." I was into it now!

"'A thief stole a woman's bike off her porch,'" I continued.

"'A vandal damaged a tractor-mower on Cunningham Road by driving it into a ditch.'"

"And, 'Deputies received a report of two people yelling near the creek.' Ha!" I chuckled to myself, wondering if it was me and Buddy hollering as we flew over the creek on the Yamaha. It would've been so cool if he'd been thinking the same thing, but I couldn't tell from the look on his face.

"'A burglar stole a mountain bike from a garage on Poplar Way.'"

"Gee, these wouldn't be crimes in Chicago," I cried. "These would be good things! A burglar steals a woman's bicycle but leaves behind the stereo and television!"

That cracked everyone up, including Buddy. He looked so cute when he laughed like that.

"Yep," chuckled Dennis, "it sure isn't Chicago."

89

"It sure isn't," I declared. "The only things you have to worry about here are your bicycles and fishing poles. Good thing all those bikes of yours are hidden in that shack in the woods, Buddy. Nobody'll ever find 'em out there."

I knew I'd made a big mistake as soon as I said it. Had I kept on reading, maybe nothing would've happened. But I stopped, wondering if I there was something I could say to erase my mistake.

"What shack in the woods?" asked Dennis.

I lowered the paper a few inches, just enough to steal a look at Buddy's face across the table. His head was down, but I could see that he was scowling. Then he raised his eyes, and I froze. I don't think anyone had ever looked at me like that. The anger in his eyes seemed to blaze a hole right through me.

Gulping hard, I raised the newspaper to cover my face.

"What bikes? What shack in the woods?" asked Dennis again.

"Yeah, what's the big secret?" said Beanie, glancing back and forth between me and Buddy.

In my mind, I kicked her hard under the table for butting in. In reality, I shrank behind the newspaper, unable to think of a single thing to say. The room was suddenly filled with this big uncomfortable silence, broken only by the sound of Marie clearing her throat.

"I don't know," Buddy finally mumbled. "I guess she must mean the bikes we keep in that little shed out back behind the house."

I took a deep breath, trying to keep my hands and the newspaper from shaking. "Yeah, that's right," I said, trying to sound sure of myself. "That shed out back . . . I guess it's not exactly out in the woods, is it?"

To my own ears, I didn't sound very convincing. I sounded like a liar, and I was sure I looked like one, too. So I didn't dare show my face. I didn't lower the shield. I wondered if Buddy could burn a hole in the paper with the look in his eyes. Sure, I'd broken my promise, but I hadn't meant to do it.

I stayed hidden behind the newspaper, pretending to read, as Buddy silently cleared his plate from the table and headed upstairs to his room.

The rest of us got into a game of hearts, but I didn't really enjoy it. I was too bummed out. I'd probably ruined everything. All because of one lousy mistake.

Could the McBeans tell that I'd lied? That Buddy and I'd both lied about the shack? I didn't think so, but I still didn't like it—I'd never lied to them before.

It was my turn. I threw down a pair of jacks but my mind wasn't on it. Instead, suddenly, I saw a couple of kids, Buddy and me, standing on the McBeans' front porch. I was dripping wet. Buddy was telling his parents a story. It was a made-up story, and I was nodding my head. I didn't feel good then, either.

TEN

I SAT STRAIGHT UP IN BED, right out of a sound sleep, scared out of my wits and gasping for air. Then, blinking and swallowing, I saw where I was and knew I wasn't dead. I'd had a terrible dream, but it was quickly swept away by an immense wave of relief and happiness. I was alive!

Letting my head fall back onto the pillow, I closed my eyes. Once again I was struggling to stay afloat in deep water, encircled by big grayish walls of granite towering above me. What was it—a canyon, a quarry? Next to me in the water was a big yellow dog, swimming for its life. The more we both struggled, the more the water seemed to churn. I tried to hang on to a rock but couldn't, then the canyon wall itself, but it was slippery, like glass. I wanted to scream, but my jaw froze shut. I knew I was going to die.

I opened my eyes again, glad to be alive, but I was horrified by the dream. I could *feel* the cold water, *feel* myself slipping away, see the poor yellow dog in the water beside me. I shivered and pulled the covers up to my chin. Then I remembered the scene at the kitchen table the night before and felt even worse.

I'd broken my promise to Buddy, but I hadn't meant to at all. It was just a mistake. It'd just slipped out. I tried to talk myself out of feeling so bad. Buddy McBean was sure to get over it. He was sure to like me again. But I'd gone to bed feeling bad, and I'd awoken feeling awful.

I rolled onto my stomach, letting my left arm dangle over the side of the bed. However Buddy had been feeling about me—I was now certain it was over. Forget more rides on his Yamaha. He'd never ask me. How could I have been so stupid, so careless?

Suddenly I missed my own room.

I missed my own mother.

Startled by the feel of something soft and wet on my hand, I lifted my head. It was Hula, licking my fingers. "Hi, girl," I whispered. "I guess you still like me, don't you?"

I kept my head up, trying to hear who was home. If Hula was up here, did that mean Buddy was home, too? That he hadn't already left for the day?

"Where's Buddy?" I whispered. "Is Buddy downstairs?" Hula wagged her tail and let out a whimper. I hoped it was a "no," because I dreaded the thought of seeing him and of ever seeing that furious look on his face again.

I lifted my arm, which felt heavy, and ran my hand through the fur around Hula's collar. She inched closer, until her head was on my pillow, her cold nose wet against my cheek. *Poor yellow dog in the water beside me.* The dog in the dream was Mambo. I was sure of it. Poor Mambo, swimming for her life. *I knew I was going to die.*

I shuddered, then rolled over and sat up, scanning the floor around the bed for my sweats. My stomach seemed a bit queasy and my head felt like a block of concrete.

"It might be the flu," I said to Hula, planting my feet on

the floor as I listened for voices, for footsteps. I couldn't hear anything and got up out of bed and into my sweats. I grabbed the blanket from the bed, too, and threw it around my shoulders, then tiptoed through the hallway and down the stairs.

Beanie, looking much like her old self, was munching on a doughnut and reading a magazine out on the deck. Rubbing my eyes as I emerged into the bright sunlight, I found a chair and plopped down into it.

"Hey, Sleepyhead," said Beanie. "It's late."

"Is it?"

"Doughnuts are in the kitchen. Dad went out and got 'em before he left for work."

"Thanks but no thanks. I'm not hungry." I squinted into the hot sunlight, my mouth dry, my throat scratchy. "I think I've got the flu."

"The *flu?*" She lifted her head in surprise. "You're kidding? The first day I feel good and you're sick?"

"Yeah, darn it. Looks that way."

"You been throwing up?"

"No."

"Got the runs?"

"No."

"I don't think you have the flu, then, Madison."

"Feels like it. I have a bad stomachache, for one thing."

"We *ate* too much yesterday, Maddie. We *ate* ourselves across the whole city."

I began to feel pouty. After all I'd done to make her feel better all week, she had the nerve to sound cross with me for not feeling well for one morning.

"It's not what I ate. It's a bug or something, and it usually takes me several days to get over it. I'm sorry about that thing at the beach," I said flatly.

"The *beach?*" said Beanie, appearing both aghast and crestfallen in the very same second. "You already know you won't be able to go to the beach on Saturday? After my parents just said we can go? You're kidding, right?"

"I wish I were. But my stomach . . ." I flattened my hand across it and frowned.

"I know! It's your period. I feel that way all the time when I've got mine."

"Sorry. No period, Beanie."

She heaved her chest and took a mini bite of her doughnut. Sometimes I hated watching her eat, the way she nibbled away at something like a little vermin. I turned my head and looked away, out over the tops of the trees, over the gold-and-green hills all the way to the sea.

"You're sure lucky to live here," I said. "You ought to stop complaining about every little thing that doesn't go your way."

"Huh?" she said, looking stunned and hurt. "That's a lame thing to say first thing in the morning."

"It just seems like you complain a lot, that's all," I said rather weakly. "It's just something I've been wanting to mention."

"Maybe you're not sick. Maybe you're just in a really bad mood."

"I am sick," I quickly replied. "But, well, I had a bad dream, too, and it creeped me out. So maybe I'm not in the best mood, either."

"I hate that. What was it about?"

I thought about telling her, then knew I couldn't, not after our fight about the quarry. "I've forgotten most of it. You look a lot better today."

"I feel a lot better. In fact, I feel great. I'm even looking forward to tomorrow, believe it or not."

"Hmph," I grunted.

"You know Buddy will be really disappointed if we aren't able to go."

"I don't think so," I said miserably.

"Yeah he will. He really likes you—I can tell—and he doesn't like many people. I ought to know, being one of them."

Hearing that only made me feel worse. I'd really blown a good thing. "He won't mind if I'm not there tomorrow. *Trust* me on this one, Beanie. I know what I'm talking about."

"Okay, okay. Well, *I'll* be disappointed if we're not able to go. I guess we've switched sides, haven't we?"

"It's Ivan, isn't it? He's cute."

"Yeah, so he's cute. So what?"

"You look like you've been caught with your hand in the cookie jar. It's okay to like somebody, you know. And I really wish we could go tomorrow, so I won't feel like I'm ruining things for you, too. But I'm sick. In fact, I'm going back to bed in a second. I can't stay out here. It's too hot."

"I bet it is. Wool is for winter." She looked at me, still wrapped in a blanket, sadly shaking her head. "We probably did too much yesterday. That's all. You rest up. I'll give you something to perk you up. When I'm done with my doughnut."

Perk me up? Beanie could be stubborn. I didn't want to get

into a tug-of-war over the knot in my stomach. She could try to perk me up if she wanted, but I knew when I was sick and when I wasn't. The truth was, I didn't mind being sick. I was glad I had the flu. I was glad I had an excuse to stay in my room.

"Where is Buddy, anyway?"

"I don't know. C'mon, we'll set you up on the couch."

She popped to her feet and went inside, carefully transporting her grossly pecked-to-shreds doughnut between two fingers.

I soon discovered what Beanie meant by "perk you up." First a glass of ginger ale because it was better for you than the citric acid in orange juice on an empty stomach. When this didn't help, she told me to try burping. I refused but agreed to a cup of bitter ginger tea, which made me gag uncontrollably. This sent Beanie to yanking books from the living-room bookshelves until she located a particular book of her mother's on miraculous cures for various ailments.

I was lying under the wool blanket on a living-room sofa, a magazine open in front of me. I lifted my eyes. Beanie was standing in front of me, a yellow raincoat in one hand and a banana in the other.

"Don't tell me," I said with great apprehension.

"It's the color yellow. It's supposed to settle the stomach. I could make you some squash, too, if this doesn't work, but I'm sure that it will."

I didn't have time to say no. She grabbed my hand and pulled me up off the sofa. In two seconds I was back down on the sofa, wearing the yellow raincoat, peeling a large and very yellow banana.

We read magazines. Beanie checked on my condition

every few minutes. Soon I began to get hot inside the rain-coat. I fanned my face with my hand. We talked about the color yellow. Wasn't it also the color of fear? I said. Like when you called somebody yellow for being a chicken? If yellow settled the stomach, I said, what color would most likely upset it? I said purple. She said green, which made the most sense. It was green, I said. That's exactly how I'd been feeling.

I was leafing through the pages of an old *Teen* magazine. Awesome beaches and very cute guys, but I had a hard time concentrating. I kept glancing at Hula, asleep on the floor beside me. *Next to me in the water was a big yellow dog, swimming for its life.*

"Is it working?" asked Beanie.

"I can't tell. I'm so hot. This seems really stupid."

"It's right in the book. I can read it to you if you like. They wouldn't put it in the book if it didn't really work, would they?"

"I guess not."

"We'll give it another half hour," said Beanie.

I nodded and looked at the page in front of me, but I didn't see what was on it. Instead, I saw Buddy looking angry at me from across the table.

"I forgot one little thing." Beanie got up and went to the kitchen.

Don't make a big thing out of nothing, I said to myself. He had a right to be mad. You did a very dumb thing, and he's sure to get over it.

"Here, this'll clinch it," said Beanie. She held her hands behind her back.

"Let me guess. Are we switching colors or still going with yellow?"

"This time the color is not important. It's in the essence of the item itself. Now don't overreact. It's says right here in the book that it really works. Ready?"

"Oh, no, you don't. I can smell it from here. Get whatever it is away from me, Beanie! You're going too far."

She made a face, either as a reaction to what I'd said or to the half-onion she held in each hand. "If you don't try, you'll ruin our whole weekend!"

I waved the magazine back and forth in front of my face, trying to cool myself off. "This is really lame, Beanie. You want me to throw up one of those onions to prove I have the flu?"

"You don't have to eat them, Madison," she said calmly. "You just put one half under each arm . . ."

"*You* put one under each arm! Get those things away from me!" I wrapped the yellow raincoat tightly around me, clenching my teeth.

Beanie glared at me, holding her ground. I glared at the onions.

"I have the flu, Beanie. You try putting an onion under your arm when you have the flu. See if it makes you feel better."

"It's in the book, Maddie."

"So's the yellow raincoat. And it hasn't been much of a success, has it?"

"Just try it. Ten minutes. You didn't come all the way to California to lie in bed with the flu. I've always admired you because you're so brave. Usually you'll try anything."

She knew how to get me. I grabbed half an onion, gritted my teeth, and shoved it under the raincoat, under my T-shirt, right into the old armpit. Ahhh, the onion was cold. It felt good under my arm. I tried not to look happy. I took the other half and did the same. Then I grabbed the remote control to the television, poked the "on" button, and sank back into the sofa.

"Ten minutes," I said. "And that's it." I looked at the clock on the mantel. One thirty-five.

Beanie came to sit beside me on the sofa. "I think this'll do it. What's on?"

"I don't know. An old movie." I sighed.

"I love old movies."

"Good. You can watch it. I've got a fever. I'll be going back to bed in a couple of minutes." I felt like a big sweathog, all rolled up and boiling hot inside the stupid yellow raincoat. Sweat beaded my forehead and drizzled down my face, but I couldn't wipe it. Raise an arm, lose an onion.

"I'm really sorry you're sick, Madison. But it would be a shame if you gave up so fast. A real rotten shame." She rubbed her nose and sniffed, scooting a few inches sideways. I could smell it, too. It was like the inside of a small greasy diner. The onions were cooking.

The back door opened—"Anyone home?"—and slammed shut behind Buddy.

I turned, frying Beanie with a look that just sizzled. "Nice going," I hissed. "I thought you said he was gone."

She shrugged.

I had no time to wriggle out of the raincoat and no time to run. I could hear Buddy's steps on the tile floor as he crossed the kitchen to the living room. I braced myself. Swallowing hard, I gulped some air and glued my eyes to the television.

I saw him enter the room out of the corner of my eye. I saw him plant his feet and dig his hands into the back pockets of his jeans.

"Hey, what's up?"

I squinted at the TV screen, didn't turn my head.

"The sun," said Beanie.

"Funny," said Buddy. "Sort of. Hey, look who's joined the fire department."

Maybe I was supposed to laugh, and maybe I wasn't. I couldn't have. My face was frozen.

He was wearing some sort of a surfing T-shirt. Still gorgeous.

"Hi, Buddy," I murmured.

"Hi, Madison. You must know something I don't know. It's blazing hot out there and not a monsoon in sight. You guys tuned to the weather channel or what?"

Beanie snorted. I squirmed on the sofa, hugging my sides.

It seemed like a miracle, the way he'd changed back to how he'd been before last night. No hate, no anger, at least not that I could see.

"Your face is so red," said Buddy to me. "Are you all right?" He threw his head back and guzzled soda from a can.

I nodded, pressing my lips together in a thin wavery smile. If I opened my mouth, I knew I would cry from relief.

"It's passion," said Beanie. "She's in love."

My eyes began to water. Maybe it was the onions, but I really didn't think so.

"Is she?" said Buddy, leaning into the wall with his right shoulder. "With whom is she in love?"

"It's a secret," said Beanie.

"Well, I can keep a secret," said Buddy. "Try me."

I could, too, and I hoped for another chance to prove it. But now I could feel the water welling up in my eyes, then two big teardrops spilling over the rim and onto my cheeks.

"Hey," said Buddy. "We were just kidding. Really. Weren't we, Beanie?"

"Yeah," said Beanie. "Just kidding."

I nodded. It was the best I could do.

Buddy took a step toward me and stopped, sniffing the air.

I stunk. The onions were slipping. I clutched my arms to my sides in a last-ditch effort.

"What is that smell? You got something cooking?" asked Buddy. "I hope."

"Nope, but I smell it, too," said Beanie, holding her nose. "What *is* it?"

"I don't know," said Buddy, "but please pass the ketchup."

Before he left the room, he looked me directly in the eye. I knew what he was trying to say, that we were all right, or I was all right, or something like that. The fear and nervousness drained right out of me, like somebody had pulled a plug. The old Buddy would've got his revenge. This new Buddy might give me another chance.

He was tramping up the stairs to his room when the onions slipped down my sides. "You know," I said to Beanie, "I really, really don't remember running home from the quarry that day."

"Isn't that strange?" said Beanie. "Because there the two of you were, all out of breath from running all that way after losing Mambo, just like I said the last time."

"I know."

"We don't have to fight about it again, do we?"

"No, Beanie. We don't."

"How do you feel, Maddie?"

"Really, really stinky."

"I bet you feel a little bit better, though, don't you?"

She didn't have a clue, and I didn't feel like telling her. What would I say? I feel much better now because your brother isn't mad at me for nearly blowing his big secret, and I've got this big crush on him?

"A little," I admitted.

"Good. Thank me later."

I had a talk with myself in the downstairs bathtub. So Buddy has a bad temper, I said. Get over it. A lot of people have tempers. Go back to having a good time and forget about whatever's stuck in your mind from the past. Time marches on. Time to get over it.

The talk didn't work. I could wash away the stinky onions, but not how I was feeling. The truth was, I didn't like Buddy's behavior the night before, and I didn't like how it made me feel. It seemed like the old days.

I studied my toes peeking up out of the water. "Buddy McBean, who are you?" I whispered.

I slid down into the tub until the water was up to my neck. Usually I liked to slip down farther, holding my nose and tilting my head back, going all the way under. I was about to do that, until I remembered my dream.

ELEVEN

I WOKE UP SATURDAY MORNING feeling much better, no stomachache, no headache, and in a much more positive mood about everything, including Buddy. That sweet, forgiving look he'd given me yesterday in the living room had stayed with me. I hadn't forgotten how he'd acted at the table that night, but it seemed time I took my own advice and gave people second chances. He was giving me one, after all.

I shifted my thinking to what I would take to the beach, to what you would take if you were fifteen or sixteen, like the kids I was going with. Did you wear your swimming suit or carry it rolled up in your towel? Would you stuff your towel in a backpack or throw it into the trunk of your car? What about sunscreen? Sunglasses? Magazines? Sneakers or thongs?

I didn't see Buddy until about noon Saturday morning, when he finally stumbled down the stairs still groggy from sleep. According to Beanie, something weird had happened on Friday night. Buddy was supposed to be working, but when Dennis and Marie popped into the restaurant for a bite to eat after some meeting, they couldn't find him. Shift change at the last minute, Buddy told them when he came home late Friday night. Said he'd gone over to a friend's house to play pool.

"Pool, my eye," said Beanie as we packed our stuff. "My parents are so stupid."

"I doubt it. But if they are, let's be grateful. If he was in trouble with your parents, we might not be going to the beach at all." I scowled. It wasn't the sort of thing I wanted to hear about Buddy just then, but I tried not to let it totally bum me out.

By early afternoon, we were on our way to the beach. Buddy drove. Augie and Hula sat up front, and Ivan rode in the back between me and Beanie, his long brown arms and legs taking up half the space in the car. I'd never gone off in a car full of kids without an adult, and I felt so cool. I knew I'd tell the story in detail to kids back home.

I was really looking forward to the day, but I still had these other feelings I couldn't shake. I was just kind of uneasy, as though I somehow knew the day could go either way. It could be a day I'd never forget or one I would want to. I told myself these feelings were nothing more than my parents whispering in my ear across the miles, telling me to be careful whenever I left the house.

We had a blast on the twenty-minute ride down to the beach, blaring the music, singing along, hanging out the windows. Buddy seemed in a good mood, too, and every so often I could feel him looking at me in the rearview mirror. I pretended not to notice, but once our eyes met and I couldn't help smiling.

The parking lot was only half full, and as soon as we

tumbled from the car and felt the change in temperature, we figured that to be the reason. It was much cooler at the beach than it'd been back at the McBean house, and I tried not to feel too disappointed.

The long path from the parking lot down to the beach cut through a wild-looking marshland. Birds floated and swooped over our heads. Tall tufts of grass sprouted up from the shallow water. High above us, two red-tailed hawks circled gracefully.

"Who do you think is cuter, Ivan or Augie?" Beanie asked, leaning toward me in a whisper as we trailed the three guys up ahead.

I looked at the two of them marching alongside Buddy in their Giants baseball caps, T-shirts, and baggy shorts. How could you tell them apart?

"No, Beanie, the question is who do *you* think is cuter? And I guess we know the answer. It's the one carrying the big bags of potato chips, and I'm going to keep an eye on him. He looks to me like somebody with a big appetite."

"I'm not interested in anyone, Maddie. I was just wondering what you thought."

"Well, I think the one you're not really interested in is just as uninterested in you, if you know what I mean."

"Silly," she said.

I *was* silly. I started talking to the back of Buddy's head.

You're so cute, I said silently. If you think I'm cute, too, then turn around and look at me. A few seconds later he did. He turned and looked at me and smiled, and I smiled right back. What more of a sign could I ask for? He liked me, and I liked him.

I have a boyfriend in California. I heard myself say this to my friends back home. It gave me shivers. It would be so cool.

I heard that other voice, too, saying, *Remember the quarry, don't forget about the quarry.* I hated that voice. It spoiled things. It frightened me. It was probably just a part of my old scared ten-year-old kid self. I looked at Hula, prancing along beside Buddy, wriggling her happy butt to and fro. See how much she loves him. But Mambo had loved him, too. *Let sleeping dogs lie,* I silently insisted.

Inside my backpack were a beach towel, a lightweight sweatshirt, sunscreen, a chicken sandwich without mayonnaise ("No mayonnaise in the sun," I'd heard my father remind me.), a Clif bar, and an apple. I should've ditched the sunscreen and gone for the mayonnaise. The closer we got to the ocean, the cooler it was getting. A smokey gray ribbon of fog lay across the horizon, like the boogeyman waiting to get you.

"If Buddy's friends hate us," murmured Beanie, grabbing my hand, "let's go off on our own."

Right at that moment, I didn't *want* to hold hands with Beanie, afraid Buddy would turn around and see us strolling along hand in hand like a couple of third graders.

"Why would they hate us?"

"Because they're older. Because they're friends of Buddy's, and he's probably said things about me."

"I doubt it. Ivan and Augie don't seem to hate us."

"But we don't know these other kids," she quietly insisted.

"No, but you are Buddy's sister. That has to count for something, doesn't it?"

She turned a sober-looking face to me and said, "Like what?"

In that moment, I felt sorrier for Beanie than I'd ever felt. That she'd think people would hate her before she'd even met them. No, the move hadn't been good for Beanie at all; it had cut her self-confidence right in half.

I gave her hand a good squeeze and hung on, not caring a heck if somebody saw us.

"Maybe if you expect to have a good time, you will. And if you expect people to like you, they will." It didn't seem like much to offer, but it was all I could think of to say.

I was probably the one who had something to worry about. Who was I? An eighth-grade graduate from La Grange, Illinois.

I held Beanie's hand for a few more seconds, then squeezed it again and let go.

Up ahead, the guys had begun tossing a football around. "Look, Ivan's showing off," I whispered, ribbing Beanie with my elbow. "I think he's trying to impress you, Beanie."

"Oh, I don't *think* so . . ."

"I do," I insisted. "And he seems really sweet." I didn't know for sure if Ivan liked her, but I hoped so. I liked to think that somebody nice here in California would go for Beanie. Maybe it would make up for having a big brother like Buddy.

When we hit the beach, I looked around for the scene from *Seventeen* magazine. I didn't see anything like it, though—just families and dogs and some kids playing Frisbee. I was surprised when we hung a left and kept on walking. And walking and walking. With a bum leg, it seemed like forever, but maybe it was only a half hour.

I should've figured. Buddy never did anything the easy way. You did something with Buddy, you took your chances, like my wild ride on the Yahama.

The sand on the beach was soft, making it extra hard to pick up your feet and keep going. The beach itself was fabulous, wide as a prairie and clean as snow except for the stuff that washed up—driftwood, seaweed, clam shells, fishnet, and so on. We saw two turkey vultures with big red rings around their eyes feasting on the guts of a dead sea lion and dozens of birds with pencil-thin beaks skidding across the sand like little roadrunners.

The small scrubby hills that separated the beach from the inland area rose higher and steeper as we got closer to Sculptured Beach. In some places, the cliffs were dissected by narrow canyons or by small mazelike caves that I wished we had more time to explore.

We crossed a couple of shallow creeks that ran down to the beach from the canyons. One creek was fairly wide and we—or Beanie, I should say—had some trouble getting across. The rest of us had made it, but she was still on the other side, searching for just the right spot to cross over.

"For Pete's sake, Beanie, it's not the Grand Canyon," growled Buddy. "Just pick a place, will ya? We haven't got all day."

"I'm trying. I just don't want to slip on the rocks."

"She must've been adopted," Buddy joked to his friends.

Beanie heard him. I saw her face fall and looked away. Darn that Buddy, anyway.

"I'll count to three," said Buddy. "Then you're on your

own. We'll go on without you. One ..."

Beanie found a spot where the water barely covered the slimy green rocks and got ready to jump. You shouldn't hesitate when you're going to do something like that. If you do, it becomes a lot harder.

"Two ..."

"Shut up, Buddy." She pursed her lips, narrowed her brow in concentration, and took a step backward.

"Thr ..."

It was a good jump. She should have made it, but at the last second, her left foot slipped back into the water. "Oh, shoot!" she cried, grabbing Ivan's outstretched hand as he pulled her forward.

"Oh, shoot!" Buddy mimicked. He sounded just like her. I almost had to laugh, but I didn't, even though he looked like he wanted me to. I was too embarrassed for Beanie.

"Maybe you should try not to do things that antagonize your brother so much," I said to Beanie a short while later. "You know how he is."

"Gee, whose side are you on, anyway?"

"I'm not on anybody's side, Beanie. This isn't a war. I'm just trying to help you have a better time. That's all. Just try a little harder."

It wasn't the whole truth. I had high expectations for our day at Sculptured Beach, and I didn't want Beanie to ruin it, by accident or not.

"Well, thanks," she said, turning her head to look at me. "I will try."

I could see tears in her eyes, and this confirmed my suspicion that I was enjoying myself more than she was my arm around her shoulder and gave it a squeeze.

By the time we hit Sculptured Beach, the beach had narrowed to a strip of sand, with immense yellow cliffs rising straight up to heaven on one side and the ocean roaring and breaking on the other. This was the wild California I'd dreamed of. Flat inky-black rocks big as my backyard at home jutted out into the sea.

By now the wind had picked up, and the fog was definitely rolling inland. I kept my fingers crossed, hoping the fog would hold back long enough for us to get in some sun and maybe a couple of games of volleyball. Just ahead of us, we saw a fire blazing in a small inlet and heard music blaring from a boom box. I saw some guys playing Frisbee and some other kids standing around the fire.

"Hey!" Buddy hurled the football. A guy in baggy purple shorts turned and caught it.

"Is that us?" I said to Beanie. I was afraid so, but I hoped not.

"Yeah," said Beanie. "And, see? They're all older."

"So what?" I replied. But it wasn't what I was thinking. It didn't look at all like a scene from *Seventeen* magazine; but these were Buddy's friends, and I wanted them to like me. I wondered if one of the girls had a crush on Buddy, or maybe was even his girlfriend. I scanned the circle. This is what it will be like going to high school, I thought. All these older kids who know each other. And how will I know how to act?

Right off the bat, I could see one girl giving me the once-over, and it really made me nervous. For a while I kept my head down, studying the tops of my sneakers. Then I noticed that, besides Beanie, I was the only one wearing them. Everyone else had bare feet or wore sandals. I made up my mind not to let it get to me. I had to be an example to Beanie.

I was standing next to a guy named Jason, who teased me for being a midwesterner, but there wasn't anything mean about the teasing, and I laughed along. A couple of the kids made fun of California, too. They said if I wanted to come to California again, I should just join the Red Cross. I asked why, stuffing my hands into the pockets of my shorts to keep from shivering. The water had changed from a vivid cobalt blue to a somber grayish green, a color I'd never seen in the ads in any magazines.

"Fires, earthquakes, floods, landslides, tsunamis . . ." (Who was Sue Nami? I wondered.) They rattled off the disasters like items on a grocery list. It was really funny. These kids weren't so bad.

"You could probably make a trip out here with the Red Cross every few weeks," said one guy. "And they'll pay your way."

"Who's Sue Nami?" I asked.

That girl who'd given me the once-over burst out laughing. "*Sue Nami?*" she repeated. I saw how cute she was, and how cute she thought she was. "A tsunami is a big, big girl wave that follows an earthquake and wipes out whole cities." She spoke as though I were eight years old. I only laughed along so I wouldn't be left out. I didn't like her a bit.

Buddy was still tossing the football around, but now he came over to stand by the fire. I could feel him watching me, and I figured I knew what he was thinking—that he had started to like me a little, but up against these older girls, he could see it was a bad idea.

The girl I didn't like asked me how old I was. I opened my mouth, but the word *thirteen* caught in my throat. I just couldn't say it. "Fourteen," I lied, wriggling my bare toes in the sand. I heard Beanie's head turn. *Don't you dare*, I silently warned.

"Oh, how sweet. A freshman. You must be really excited."

I felt about two feet tall, but I swallowed my insecurity and gave the girl a hard, steady look, trying to hold my own, for my sake and Beanie's.

"Not that excited," I mumbled. "But I am looking forward to my trip to Europe next summer." I gazed into the fire and said a little prayer, hoping nobody would ask me anything. I had had no idea I was going to say such a thing, and if somebody had asked me where in Europe I was going, I might have said something really stupid, like Iowa City.

Nobody asked me, though. Somebody said cool, and that was all. Lying was easy, a lot easier than looking stupid in front of Buddy and the rest of his gang.

Beanie tittered beside me, and I realized she knew the truth and wasn't saying anything. Smart Beanie! The girl across the fire didn't say another word.

Ivan tossed the football to Beanie. It struck her in the ribs and landed with a thud in the sand. He laughed, but it wasn't a mean laugh. Angel Ivan, I said to myself, as I bent to pull a sweatshirt from my backpack. Then I felt a tap on my shoulder. I turned and looked up. It was Buddy.

"Go for a walk?"

"Me?"

"No, your aunt Mabel. Yeah, you."

I smiled up at him, but I didn't immediately jump to my feet. I hesitated, then saw his surprise. I suppose most girls didn't waste a second after an invitation from Buddy.

"Sure," I finally answered, slowly getting to my feet. "Just a second. Let me tell Beanie." It seemed like the right thing to do, given my agreement to stick together, but I could tell that he didn't like it.

"Hey, Beanie," I said, stepping away. "I was thinking of going for a walk with your brother."

"What?" She looked at me in surprise, too.

"I'm sure we won't be gone that long," I added, trying to sound reassuring. "Just for a walk down the beach."

Beanie's gaze drifted from me to Buddy, who was kicking a hole in the sand behind me. "Sure, go ahead," she said with a shrug.

"You're sure? I can stay if you want. Really, I can." I hated to leave her behind, but I really did want to go.

"Best friend or baby-sitter?" Buddy mumbled behind me. I pretended not to hear.

"No, go ahead. I'll be all right," said Beanie. She tried to smile before turning away.

It must've been hard for her, seeing Buddy maybe liking me when he didn't seem to like her. I knew she wouldn't hold it against me, though. She just wasn't like that.

I didn't think anyone would blame me for going off with a guy this good-looking. Well, maybe my mother. But not any of the girls in this group, as far as I could tell from the glances I got as Buddy and I began to head down the beach.

Sometimes things just happen the way they're supposed to, and you shouldn't interfere.

TWELVE

THAT GRAY BAND OF FOG along the horizon had doubled in size, which I took to mean it was heading inland. The wind had picked up, too. I'd started out with my sweatshirt tied around my waist, but now I stopped to slip it on over my head. Buddy could endure the cold in a T-shirt if he wanted, but I had no need to prove a thing.

A couple of really cute girls in the group and he'd asked *me* to go for a walk. I could almost imagine what it would feel like to be Buddy's girlfriend. To go places with a guy this good-looking and popular.

"Hey, Hula, don't get lost on us," hollered Buddy. "We might be needing you as a chaperon."

I turned red and didn't dare look at him. What was he planning?

"I didn't know you were going to Europe next summer. You turning into a rich kid or what?"

"No," I said with an embarrassed little laugh. "You should talk!" I knew I was about to be caught in a lie. That what I'd said would get back to his parents and then back to mine. "It's not a sure thing," I explained. "It's highly likely I'll never get to go."

"Well, I hope you do. We can rendezvous in Paris or Rome, and we can ride around Europe on my Yamaha."

"Huh," I mumbled, sounding stupid and bored. I wasn't. I just couldn't believe this tall, good-looking guy was saying this to me. My mind flashed to this movie I'd seen about a guy and a girl meeting on a train from Paris to Vienna, and what a great, romantic time they had roaming the city together all night long.

"If you yawn right now, I'll have a nervous breakdown," said Buddy.

I laughed, but I knew my ears turned red. I was like a human rainbow with this guy, chicken yellow to crimson and purple. Every so often, as we walked side by side down the beach, I would catch him looking at me, or he'd catch me sneaking a look at him, and we'd smile and look away. Yes, maybe I could have a boyfriend.

The beach soon narrowed even more until it was only about three feet wide, bounded by the ocean and a rugged landscape of rock-strewn coves and inlets, caves and sea tunnels partially filled with water. It was magnificent. As we hopped among the slippery black rocks, peering everywhere, I kept checking on Hula, but she seemed more surefooted than I, and just as elated. Both Buddy and I would have liked to further explore the caves and tunnels, but the tide seemed on its way in, and we weren't sure we'd have enough time. I didn't know much about the ebb and flow of tides, but with the cliffs towering above us on one side and the ocean roaring and battering the rocky shore on the other, I knew it wasn't a place I'd ever want to be trapped.

A couple of times, as we were hopping the rocks, wandering here and there, he held out his hand and I took it. His hand was warm, and softer than I would have expected. I didn't take his help as a sign he thought I was incapable or clumsy. I took it to mean he didn't want anything bad to happen to me. I wondered what he'd have done if I'd been his sister, if he would have held out his hand or just let her fend for herself.

Right when we were about to turn back, we came to a narrow canyon carved out of the side of a cliff. Soon I was following Buddy along a narrow trail that wound around the brown hills on the back side of the cliffs. Buddy called this trail a switchback. I liked the sound of the word, and I liked walking behind him. I could stare at the back of his head, the hair a little scruffy on his neck, and wonder what was going on inside it, if any of his thoughts were about me.

We saw a mother rabbit and four or five little babies along the way and often heard the sounds of other small animals scurrying for cover. I wondered what else was out here. Buddy said foxes and bobcats—and he didn't want to frighten me, but there were occasional sightings of mountain lions, too. "Well, we've got Hula," I said.

"Right," he said laughing. "She'll take care of us both."

By the time we stopped to catch our breath, we'd already been gone longer than I'd expected, and I felt a bit guilty about being away from Beanie for so long. At certain points on the switchback, I could see our group down below on the beach, growing smaller and smaller. Well, going down would be faster, I reasoned.

"You're a real trooper. I like that about you," said Buddy, stopping to tell me this about halfway up. "No complaining, no whining about how tough the trail is. That's really cool."

"Gee, thanks," I said with a shrug.

Funny he should say that right then, because it was getting harder and harder to pick up my feet and keep going. And not because I was tired, though I was. I was anxious, and the closer we got to the top, the more fearful I felt. I really didn't understand it. Maybe being away from home was harder on me than I thought. Maybe it was making me a little crazy or causing me to backslide into that old self again, the one who worried about crashing. Whatever it was, it made me eager to turn around and head back.

When we got to the top, I plopped myself down cross-legged on the ground about twenty feet back from the edge of the cliff, more anxious than ever. Hula, sniffing and panting, was more interested in what might be lurking in the bushes behind us than she was in the view.

"Hey, come check out the view," Buddy hollered. "It's awesome."

"Soon as I catch my breath," I called out. I didn't want him to know how crazy I felt, how scared I was to be up here at the top. Small wisps of fog sailed over our heads. I was still warm from the hike, but my hands were freezing.

I retied the laces on my sneakers and pulled my hair back to keep it from blowing in my face. I was stalling for time, trying to figure out what was wrong with me.

"Come check it out before the fog blows in."

"Haven't we been gone a long time? You think we should head back now?"

"We're okay. Nobody's keeping time. C'mon over."

"You know, Buddy, it's really odd, but I forgot that I used

to be—and I guess I still am—well, a little afraid of heights. Not *really, really* afraid, but a little, so I think I'll just sit here while you . . ."

"Really?" he said, turning to stare. "What a bummer. Well, there's nothing to be afraid of, and I promise I'll hang on to you. You trust me that much, don't you?"

"Oh, sure," I rushed to say. "It's just . . ."

Inside, I was dying of embarrassment and humiliation. My one big chance and I was blowing it with some new phobia. What was the matter with me, anyway?

"Oh, c'mon, give it a try. You don't want to come all this way up and miss the view."

The wind rippled across his T-shirt and gently lifted the hair on his head. He was something to look at! I really wanted to trust him, too. And I wanted to go back home and tell everyone I had a boyfriend in California. So I made myself do it. I eased myself up off the ground, dusted my hands off, and ambled over to him. He grabbed my hand, and we turned toward the sea.

I'd never held hands with a boy before, not like this. You want something like that to be perfect, but it wasn't. My nerves were still tingling, for one thing.

"See?" said Buddy. "It's not so bad up here, is it?"

"No, it isn't," I murmured, keenly aware of my hand inside his. Aware, too, that we were only about a foot or so from the edge of the cliff, and that was close enough for me.

"If you lean forward a bit you can see everything. Don't worry—I've got you. Nothing bad will happen, and I won't let go of your hand."

I felt like a big baby, but I made myself do it. Bending

from the waist, I leaned forward and looked down, straight into the blue-gray sea, swirling and seething below us. Then I felt dizzy and drew in my breath.

"It's a long way down," I murmured with a shiver.

"Yeah, it sure is. Splat." He laughed.

"Yeah, right. Splat," I repeated, but it didn't sound like me saying it. I was trembling, and as I peered over the edge, I felt light-headed again. So I lifted my head and looked straight out to sea. That seemed to help. A big gray sheet of fog was sweeping its way low across the water, scary looking and yet beautiful.

"You're shivering," said Buddy. "Are you cold?"

"A little."

I thought he was going to put his arm around me, and when he didn't I was glad, because I seemed on the verge of tears, and I thought it would make me cry.

He gave my hand a squeeze instead. This made me feel small, like a little girl—a scared girl, I guess, who couldn't stop shivering, inside and out.

Right at that moment I didn't feel thirteen or fourteen or anything in between. I felt like I was about ten or eleven, standing on a ledge in the quarry, Buddy next to me in his cutoffs. *Should we jump?* he was saying.

"Awesome, isn't it?" said Buddy.

"It really is," I said, clenching my teeth to try to keep them from chattering.

He moved a bit closer to the edge, until the toes of his sneakers were almost hanging over, but I hung back, still holding on to his hand.

"Once I was up here during a heck of a storm. I could see lightning striking way out over the ocean, and the waves were about twenty feet high. I'd like to surf in something like that. Someday I will."

"Buddy," I urged. "Be careful." I had a funny feeling, a tingling at the base of my skull. Just then Hula began yelping, and I turned to look for her. Sitting back on her haunches, she had her eyes on Buddy, her brows furrowed in one of those worried-dog looks.

The quarry, said the voice in my head, louder and more insistent than ever. I now tried to take a step backward, but Buddy still had ahold of my hand.

"Hey, don't go yet," he pleaded.

"Buddy, this makes me really nervous. You're standing too close to the edge."

"According to whom?" He chuckled, running a hand through his hair. "Madison, try to loosen up a bit. Your fears aren't based on anything real, so don't let them get the best of you. Nothing bad's going to happen."

Mostly I believed him, but I didn't like that he still had ahold of my hand, which I tried to ease free without throwing either of us off balance.

"Buddy, please let go."

Hula was barking her head off. My nerves were on fire, and any second I was sure I would burst into tears.

"Hey, Hula! Pipe down! Gee," he murmured, letting go of my hand. "I didn't think you were this uptight. You were pretty cool with the Yamaha."

"Sorry!" I blurted, hating his disappointment in me. "I loved your Yamaha . . ."

The wind snapped at his hair. He scowled, hunching his shoulders.

Ask him, said the voice in my head. Ask him what? I wondered.

"Oh, forget it," Buddy mumbled. "Everybody's different. Me, someday I'm going to try hang gliding from one of these cliffs. You take a running jump and off you go. I'll do it, too." He lifted his arms like a bird, teetering on the edge of the cliff. A big gust could've blown him right over.

"Aren't you afraid of anything, Buddy?" I murmured.

"Not much that I know of."

I wanted a different answer. I wanted him to say yes, he was afraid of this or of that. Of falling or dying, of failing at something or losing someone, anything that would make him more real.

"It's just a feeling, isn't it?" I said.

"It's not one I'm big on."

"I guess I like my life, and I'd like to live more of it."

"But why bother, if that's how you're going to live it."

That hurt my feelings. I turned my head so he couldn't see.

Hula was still going wild, yelping her head off.

"Oh, hush up, Hula," snapped Buddy. But Hula wouldn't stop, not until he'd stepped away from the edge and turned to look at her.

"Silly dog," he mumbled.

Smart dog, I said to myself.

"She likes you, Buddy. She doesn't want to lose you."

It was a small smile, almost tender, and it softened his face. He dropped to his knees and snapped his fingers. "Come here, Hula. Come on, girl."

Hula dropped her head and ambled toward us, still

breathing hard from her run up the trail. She stopped where I was standing and leaned into my leg, wagging her tail.

"I guess she likes you better," said Buddy. He snapped his fingers again, commanding Hula to come right up to him.

I knew about golden retrievers. They aimed to please. Mambo was like that, too. They'd do almost anything for you. Almost.

Ask him now. I heard that voice again, loud and clear.

Hula lowered her head and inched forward. I could feel her reluctance, and I didn't blame her.

"Buddy," I suddenly blurted. "There's something I've got to ask you . . ."

"Yeah?" he said, his voice now sullen and hard. "Go right ahead."

I took a deep breath. I was shaking inside and out, and I was suddenly sick to my stomach. "I need to ask you . . . uh . . . Beanie says . . ."

"'Beanie says,'" he repeated. "This should be good. Go ahead . . ."

"I just wonder if you remember what happened at the quarry that day?"

He looked over at me in surprise. "Quarry? What day?"

"That day . . . You know, a couple of years ago . . . The day Mambo died."

"What about it?" he rasped, his eyes suddenly narrowing.

"I know Mambo drowned, but I've been having this feeling that we were there when it happened. I mean that we were there together. If I'm wrong, go right ahead and tell me. I told Beanie she was nuts, at first I mean, but now, I don't know . . ."

"How should I know? It was a long time ago."

What I wanted was a straight-out "no." Not this "How should I know?" It wasn't right. It wasn't a good answer, and I wasn't at all relieved.

"I just need to know for sure. I've been trying to remember . . ."

"Well, why don't you not try. Why don't you just forget it. What's the point?"

I didn't have one, and what I did have I couldn't begin to explain. "If I was there, I would just like to know, but I can't really remember. Beanie says . . ."

"If Beanie said it, forget it."

"I was hoping you could tell me . . ."

"You tell me. You seem to know more than I do."

The way he was snapping was hurting my feelings, but I kept going. "Beanie says . . ."

"So ask Beanie. Look, I sure didn't bring you up here to recycle the past."

"Okay," I said softly. "Sorry."

Something buried in my mind was about to shake loose. I could feel it. Beside me, Hula was still balking, sitting on her haunches.

"C'mon, Hula. C'mon, girl, you come over here right now or you're going to be sorry."

"Come on, Mambo. It's a hot day. You want to go for a swim?" I heard Buddy laugh.

Buddy lunged for Hula and missed. Then I heard more of those voices from the past, loud and clear, and I listened.

"It's okay, Mambo," he was saying, "don't be a fraidy cat. It's not that far down." Poor Mambo. She didn't want to go for a swim, and

she didn't want to jump, either. She was afraid like me. "How about you?" Buddy said to me. "You want to go for a swim with Mambo?"

I shook my head. Tears slipped down my cheeks. Poor Mambo and poor me.

"Buddy, I don't think Hula wants to come to you," I said now. "Can't you just let her be?"

"Hey! What's your problem? You're starting to sound like my bimbo sister."

I bit my lip, stung again by the tone of his voice. Then I dropped to my knees, wrapped my fingers around Hula's collar, and hung on.

I'm back at that quarry again, and I wish I wasn't because I don't like how it feels. I'm remembering what I didn't want to remember, seeing what I hadn't wanted to see. It's Buddy and me, standing on a cliff looking down into the water, and Mambo is with us. I'm frightened. How old am I? Nine? Ten?

No, I don't want to go for a dive. It's a long way down. I shake my head, but I can't say anything. My mouth is glued shut. Mambo is shrinking from Buddy, but she can't get away. He reaches for her, lifts her up into his arms. She squeals. "Don't be such a baby," says Buddy. "Mambo go for a swim." He holds her out over the water in the quarry—and lets go. I hear the big splash, and then Mambo yelping, yelping. Then nothing.

I shuddered. My hands on Hula's collar were shaking like mad.

He had killed his own dog. Maybe he hadn't meant to kill her, but he had just the same.

I blinked hard.

He had killed his own dog. And nobody knew but me.

"You look weird, and you're acting kind of weird, too,"

Buddy muttered. "What's the matter with you, anyway?"

Hula squirmed under my grip. "Easy, Hula, easy," I cooed. I was hanging on as much for me as for her. I knew she was anxious, and if I let her go she'd run. And I might just run with her.

I needed to know, though. If what I remembered had really happened, or was I just going crazy? "I . . . I think Beanie was right," I sputtered, my voice shaking badly. "I think I was with you that day,"

Buddy rose to his feet, turning away from me. "Oh, so you're still talking about the quarry."

"Yes. It was terrible, what happened, wasn't it?" I looked up at him, waiting, hoping he'd say yes, what happened was awful, and he hadn't meant to do it. It was a horrible accident. He hadn't meant to let her go.

I saw the memory flicker across his face, and for a moment he looked sad. I thought I saw a glimpse of who he could have been, then his face closed up, hardened itself around the past, and I was alone again and scared.

"Mambo, Mambo!" we shout, racing down the side of the hill. When we get to the bottom, I can see Mambo struggling out in the middle of the quarry.

"Mambo!" I shout. Mambo lifts her head and begins trying to dog-paddle toward us, but I can see how tired she is. "Buddy!" I cry. "Help her! We've got to do something!"

"She can make it," he says.

I don't think so. I pull off my shoes, jump in, and start swimming. By the time I get to her, my arms are already limp with fatigue. I'd never been that tired in the water before.

I see the awful look of terror in Mambo's big eyes. She starts to slip beneath the water just as I grab her by the collar and try to pull her along while I swim. I know how scared she is. I know that's why she gets her front paws up onto my shoulders and tries to climb onto my back. She's trying to find something to hang on to. Her nails dig into my back and shoulders. I'm too tired to cry out. She's a big dog. I can't swim and carry her too, and I start to go under myself. I turn and try to push her, try to roll her off of me with one arm, still hanging on to her collar. She fights me, though, and in her panic she's pulling me under. I'm afraid I'm going to die. I let go of her collar and push off with my feet. There is one pitiful yelp. Then I swim away, and I don't look back.

Until now. I blinked, lifting my head.

Buddy stood with his hands thrust deep into his pockets. "What's wrong with you now? You look really weird."

I loved that dog so much and could still see the terror in her eyes. Now my own eyes brimmed with tears and spilled over. I shook my head, unable to say anything. I'd nearly drowned, too, and Buddy hadn't done anything to try to help me.

He squinted, like I had gone crazy. "God, was I ever wrong about you."

I swallowed hard, stung by what that might mean about me and knowing now how wrong I'd been about him.

"I don't know why you're acting like this or what you think you remember, but you're wrong. Mambo was a good dog, and she drowned. She couldn't swim. End of story."

I looked at Buddy. I looked at him in such a way he had to know what I was thinking.

"Most dogs *can* swim," he said. "And don't forget, you were there, right? You said so yourself. You didn't do anything to stop me, did you?"

Standing next to Buddy while he holds Mambo over the water. My mouth is clamped shut. I feel the words in my throat, words that want to stop him, but they don't come out. After it's over, Buddy and I run home to tell Dennis and Marie. He stops me before we go in. I'm soaking wet. He says if I ever tell anyone what happened, I'll really be sorry, and he gives me that look, that same hateful look I saw at the kitchen table. I remember the lie Buddy tells, how Mambo and I had slipped and fallen in, and he had to choose between us. I stand right next to him, hearing him tell it, and don't say anything. My mouth is glued shut.

He was right. Maybe I had tried to save her, but I hadn't done anything to stop him. And maybe to hide my own guilt, I had forgotten it all.

I began to cry, burying my face in Hula's fur.

"You're overly dramatic," mumbled Buddy. "Always have been. Thought you'd changed, but I guess you haven't. It's a big disappointment. Let's go."

I lifted my head and wiped my eyes. "If Mambo was such a good dog," I blurted, "why'd you throw her off a cliff like a sack of potatoes?"

I expected he would deny it. I figured he would tell me I was crazy.

"To see what she was made of," he snapped. "You know the old saying 'You sink or you swim.'"

With that he rushed past me. I turned to watch him go, stunned beyond belief. Everything was different now. Everything was ruined.

"That was quite a long walk," Beanie whispered to me in the huddle.

They were all playing touch football. I joined one team, and Buddy joined the other.

You have no idea, I wanted to say, but I just nodded and said I was sorry. Maybe later I would tell her. I had to tell someone. You can't keep something like that to yourself. But what would I tell her? That she was right—I had been at the quarry with Buddy? That I'd stood by and watched while he'd thrown Mambo over the side? That I was sorry but I had forgotten?

Ivan took the snap and hurled a spiral right into my gut. When the ball came to me, I dropped it. I didn't have the heart for playing. I kept seeing Mambo, tossed over the side of the quarry like a sack of flour. Tears sprang to my eyes, and I lowered my head to brush them away. I just couldn't help it.

Beanie sidled up alongside me and asked me what was the matter. I told her it was a long story. She asked me if I was feeling sick, and I said not exactly.

Beanie took the next pass. She dropped it but quickly scooped it up and took off running. "Go Beanie!" I hollered. My voice sounded hollow, as though I were calling from inside a drum.

Poor Beanie didn't get far. Buddy quickly caught up with her, grabbing her shoulders from behind and flinging her down to the ground. Flinging her down *hard*.

He was mad. Mad at me for making him remember.

Beanie was slow getting up but no whining this time, not a word or a whimper. I could see what was happening, how hard she was trying to play well, to not irritate Buddy, to get on his good side. And maybe to impress Ivan, too. I pressed my lips together and went to give her a hand.

"Nice run there, Beanie," I said, pulling her up.

"Oh, not really," she puffed. "I guess I didn't get too far, did I?"

"You did great." I slipped my arm around her shoulder on our way back to the huddle. "I couldn't have done any better."

It happened again a couple of plays later, Buddy roughing her up like before, bringing her down harder than he needed to. This time I said something. I said, "You're too rough, Buddy," just as he was walking away. Then I said, "If you're mad at me, don't take it out on your sister."

My heart beat hard when I said this. I was still hoping he'd say the right thing. "Oh, was I too rough? Sorry." But he didn't. He turned and I saw his surprise. His eyes were big and dark, and his lips were pressed together in a grim even line.

He didn't look cute to me now. I didn't notice his blue eyes or pretty brown hair. He looked mean. He looked like a brute, and maybe that's what he was.

"Who said I'm mad? Why should I be mad?" he sneered, brushing the sand from his hands and knees. "Football's a rough game. She shouldn't be playing."

"Bully," I mumbled under my breath, turning away. He was cute and he was mean, and that was a bad combination.

"*What?*" he demanded, turning to stare.

I shrugged. "We're supposed to be playing a game. It's not boot camp."

"No, it's life. And someday she'll thank me."

"Or hate you," I said, lowering my head and turning away.

I felt him glaring as I plodded my way back to the huddle, but I didn't care. He didn't walk on water in my book.

I bit down on my lip to keep it from quivering. So much for *Seventeen* magazine. Maybe I was playing touch football on one of California's great beaches, and maybe a super song blared from the boom box. But so what? The guy I'd started to fall for was somebody I couldn't trust, a big nothing. So don't call it Paradise.

"You don't have to stand up for me," said Beanie on our way back to the huddle. "I know you have a crush on him."

"Past tense," I said. "It's over."

"Why?"

"It's a long story, Beanie. Maybe he's just a big jerk like you said."

I could see her surprise, and some irritation, too. Maybe calling your own brother a jerk doesn't make it okay for your best friend to do the same.

"Sorry." I shrugged. "It's just how I feel."

Beanie seemed and looked rather flustered, bewildered actually, and I didn't blame her. She played a pretty good game, though, better than me. I could see what she was doing, taking seriously my suggestion to not antagonize her brother. Trouble was, I was now sorry I'd said it.

THIRTEEN

I WAS SORRY I SAID IT because it was wrong. So was
I, and so was Buddy. I was wrong because I'd given Beanie
bad advice in terms of her brother, and I was wrong because
Buddy was the same old Buddy after all. Buddy was wrong
for—well, the list was too long.

I was sure we'd head back home as soon as the game was
over. I was cold, thirsty, and hungry, and I figured everybody
else was, too. I was wrong again. We were going to check out
those sea caves Buddy and I had passed on our hideous hike
up to the overlook. I didn't have any choice but to tag along.

The tide was coming in fast, so we knew we had to stop
at the first set of caves. That was fine with me. The sooner we
went back the better. I was done exploring. In fact, you
could have put me on a plane to Chicago right then and I
wouldn't have minded, because how was I going to stay in
the same house with Buddy? How would I sit at the same
table with a boy who'd thrown his own dog off a cliff? A boy
I'd started to *like*.

"C'mon, Hula. Don't you get lost. You stay with me and
Beanie, okay?" I didn't really have to tell her that. She'd left
Buddy's side and was hanging real close to me now.

The cave was situated at the rear of a small sandy cove. To get to it, you had to climb down or jump from a ledge of rocks to the sand below, then wade through knee-deep water to get to the opening. The opening was fairly big. From where I was standing, I could see inside, and it looked like you'd expect a cave to look, dark and wet, with stalactites hanging from the ceiling. It was clear that you could crawl thirty or forty feet back into the cave, then climb out through an opening in the cave's ceiling and hop back onto the rocky ledge. Had I been in a different mood, I would've been one of the first to jump down there, tide coming in or not.

I watched as Buddy and Jason dropped down to the beach below and began trudging through swirling sea water toward the mouth of the cave. Big shot, I said to myself.

"You wanna go, too?" asked Beanie.

"Doubt it," I said with a shrug. I had a wedge of disappointment lodged in the middle of my chest. It was hard to talk and hard to breath. How could I have liked somebody as mean as Buddy?

"Something's wrong with you. I can tell," said Beanie, turning to study my face. "You've been weird since your walk. What is it? What happened?"

"I can't talk about it now, Beanie. I'm sorry." I knew if I did I'd start to cry, right there in front of everyone. "I'll tell you about it later, okay?"

"I knew something was wrong. Okay, tell me later. Promise?"

"Promise." I bit down on my lower lip. Poor Dennis and Marie. It was going to hurt when they learned the truth about Buddy. They'd feel really bad too—much worse than me. Shoving my hands into the pockets of my shorts, I watched as Buddy disappeared into the mouth of the cave.

Those of us standing along the ledge were getting showered with sea spray as the ocean hammered away at a jumble of rocks not far from where we were standing. I kept ducking, covering my head with my arms. Every so often a huge wave came crashing into the sandy cove below, raising the water level by an extra foot or so before it was sucked back out to sea.

I could hear Buddy and Jason whooping it up. I hated show-offs. And I was jealous. I wasn't the wallflower type—part of me wanted to be down there, too, even after all that had happened. A few minutes later they reappeared, pulling themselves up and out of the cave through the hole in the ceiling. I turned my head. The last thing I wanted was to have Buddy catch me watching, to let him think for one second that I could still like him.

"Why don't you want to go in?"

"I don't know, Beanie. I just don't feel like it. I'm cold and wet, for one thing. I'd like to not get pneumonia, if I can possibly help it."

"You won't get pneumonia. Trust me. This is California."

"Oh, right. Nobody gets sick here in Paradise."

Augie and two of the girls went down next. As they moved slowly toward the mouth of the cave, the water crept past their kneecaps. Every few seconds a wave would roll in, pushing the water to waist-high level before being pulled back to sea. No wonder Buddy had gone first. He was no dummy. It was slower going and not so easy for the second shift.

"C'mon," said Beanie, giving the end of my sweatshirt a yank. "Let's do it. Let's go in."

"No, thanks. I said I didn't want to."

"Well, I am."

"Don't be stupid, Beanie. You can't even swim."

"So," she replied, suddenly sounding a lot like my sister. "It's not over your head. You can walk in."

"It will be! The tide's coming in. I might be a midwesterner, but I've got some common sense about stuff like this, and you should have some, too."

Beanie was watching her brother wring the water out of his T-shirt. I knew what she was thinking. Here was a chance to impress him. If she did this, maybe he would like her. Maybe he'd think she was worth his approval.

"Beanie," I said, turning and looking her right in the eye. "You know what I said about trying not to get on your brother's bad side? Well, forget it. I gave you the wrong advice. Don't try to please him, and don't try to impress him. It'll get you in trouble."

She dug her hands into the pockets of her windbreaker, frowning at the scene below. "I don't know why you're now telling me something different, but I don't want to be the only one not going in."

"*I'm* not going in. Ivan hasn't gone in."

"Listen. Everybody's laughing and having a good time, and we're just standing here watching."

"Beanie, you've got nothing to prove. Not one doggone thing."

"That's not why I'm going in. Oh, c'mon!" She turned to me and smiled, pulling off her windbreaker. Then she made a move for the rocky incline, slipping and sliding her way down to the water. She turned once and waved for me to follow. I shook my head.

I waited a few more seconds, then tried calling her back, but with the deafening roar of the surf, I was sure she hadn't heard me. I cupped my hands together and called again. *"Beanie."* Suddenly I was standing there alone, hands in my pockets, watching the water gush into the cove. You should go with her, I said to myself, but I really didn't *want* to go with her. It was the exact opposite of what I wanted to be doing. I wanted to go *back*, back to wherever Dennis and Marie were, where it was warm and safe and dry.

Occasionally I could hear a shout from inside the cavern. I hoped they were going to wait for Beanie, who was now plunging forward through water up around her thighs. Every so often she turned and flashed me a smile, waving me toward her. I tried waving her back but nothing doing. She could be so stubborn. Go after her, I said to myself; go after her *now*. But I wasn't sure it was the right thing to do. I wasn't sure I could . . .

A sudden plume of sea spray rose straight up from the rocks right in front of me, sending me scuttling backward. I heard Buddy laugh, and I turned.

"Something funny?" I snapped. Maybe it was the wrong thing to say. Maybe I should've played along with him, not thrown gas on the fire, but I was too hurt and too mad, and he was too mean, to take his teasing in a good-natured way.

"Yeah. You should see yourself."

"And why is that, Buddy?"

"Ever see a crab running backward?"

It stung. I bit down on my lip and turned away.

A head poked through the roof of the cave, wet hair plastered to the girl's face. If Buddy called Beanie back, she would come. What I needed to do was forget about myself and how I was feeling and go right up to him. Go over to him now and tell him to call Beanie back.

Beanie lurched forward, wiped out by a big one. She was having a hard time getting back on her feet, with nothing to grab on to or push off from. I had a bad feeling. Even from where I was standing, I could see that the water level in the cave had risen.

I made myself do it. I walked right over to where Buddy and the others were standing. He had his arm around the girl who didn't like me. Maybe nobody liked me now. I told myself it didn't matter.

He looked at me and I looked at him. "Well?" said Buddy.

My knees were shaking when I opened my mouth. "Don't you think you should go after your sister? You know she can't swim."

Buddy looked to his left, then his right. "What am I, the only lifeguard on duty?"

That got a few laughs. I dug my toe in the sand and waited. I wasn't as clever as Buddy. I didn't know what to say next.

"Well, I'm not on duty, and I'm not my sister's keeper. Beanie can take care of herself, just like everyone else."

"I don't think she can," I said. I blushed in spite of my anger, glancing at Ivan, who gave a helpless shrug, then couldn't seem to help peering into the cove with a look of concern.

"Tide is coming in fast, Buddy," he murmured.

"So?" said Buddy. "I've been in tidewater a lot deeper than that. If she was dumb enough to go in now, she can get herself out. You go help her if you're worried," he said to me. "You can swim, can't you?"

I looked at him straight in the eye. "You know I can." Then I whirled to my right and stormed off. He was a spineless jellyfish, and I hated him with all my heart.

I pulled off my sweatshirt and dropped it in the sand. How could I have been crushed out on such a big loser? I was furious, so furious that in that moment not even the spray of icy seawater on my bare arms and legs seemed to faze me as I began to ease my way over the rocks and down to the sea.

The fear didn't hit me until I was standing on the last rock, about to let myself drop down into the rushing water. I didn't think I could do it and took a step backward. But when I lifted my head to get my bearings, I saw Beanie down below and way ahead of me, staggering toward the cave. I did not have time to stand there and think.

I gasped as I slid down the rock, the water immediately up to my thighs and icy cold. After a few faltering steps toward the cave, I turned to look behind me. What I saw was amazing. I was eye to eye with an enormous green-gray sea, an army of whitecaps rolling toward me, the whole scene shrouded in an eerie mist. Then I had to do what Beanie's father said you should never do: I turned my back to the sea. Turned my back to it and began to will my legs toward

Beanie, who was now near the entrance to the cave.

"Beanie!" I stopped to holler.

She lifted her head and looked toward the group on the cliff, waving. I knew what she was trying to say: Look at me, Buddy! See, I'm not afraid. I'm just like you. I'm just like everybody else.

Buddy looked at me, too, and I still felt that tug of excitement. But I had something else tugging at me now, a stiff undertow that felt as though it would pull me out to sea if I didn't pay close attention. Well, I knew how to swim, but so what? That was about as helpful right now as knowing how to sail a boat in your bathtub.

How would I catch up with Beanie?

Yeooowww . . . I'd stepped on sharp rock and raised my foot in pain. When I set it back down, it slid across something slippery and I lost my footing altogether, tumbling forward and down, suddenly up to my neck in icy water. I struggled against the fierce undertow, as the fast-receding waters kept pulling my feet out from under me. Pushing off the soft sandy bottom with everything I had, I heaved myself up and staggered forward, rubbing salt water from my eyes in order to see.

I could see Ivan waving from the cliff above me. The little group was now nearly invisible, veiled in fog. But I could see Buddy's face, and it frightened me. I thought he looked scared. Then Buddy took a step toward the edge of the ledge. Ivan motioned to me with his arms. What? Come back? Go forward? Hurry up?

Ahead of me, Beanie was struggling through waist-high water. What really worried me was this: I had thought the water at the farthest end of the cove would be shallower. But it wasn't. The closer I got to the cave, the deeper the water. There was no place for the water to go, and the cove seemed to slant slightly downward away from the sea, so that the cave was actually below sea level. The water was now above my waist, and I was taller than Beanie.

Just keep going, I said to myself, you can make it. But I was having a hard time moving my legs, which were numb from the cold. I looked up at the kids on the cliff. Buddy, I wanted to say, please come get us. Please help. I picked him out, a head taller than the rest. *What am I, the lifeguard?*

I didn't have time to think about Buddy. Instead, I dove toward the cave and started to swim, pretty much dragging my legs behind me. At least I was moving. When I hit the cave I had nothing left and I knew it. My arms were like lead, and I couldn't even feel my feet or my legs. I was gasping for air, way past tired, way past any kind of tired I'd ever felt, and I couldn't see Beanie.

Inside the sea cave there was a drop-off of about a half foot. So the water was even deeper than I'd expected.

What I saw next I'll never forget. I saw Ivan with his arms extended down through the hole in the ceiling. I saw Beanie, her arms extended up toward Ivan, the water level with her chin. She was popping up and down like a buoy in heavy seas. I could guess what she was doing, pushing off the bottom with her toes, trying to grab hold of Ivan. She was missing by inches. Inches.

Behind Ivan stood Buddy, frozen in place, white as death.

My head was just above water. I could hear things, shouting, yelling, water sloshing around the inside of the cave, the inside of my ears. I could hear Ivan: "C'mon, Beanie, c'mon . . ."

C'mon, Beanie, c'mon . . . C'mon, Beanie, c'mon . . . I sang it to myself as I grabbed on to a half-submerged stalactite and pulled myself forward. C'mon, Beanie . . .

Suddenly I couldn't see anything as the water lapped up past my eyes. I clung to the stalactite with everything I had. When I opened my eyes I could see Beanie's hand. Then I lost her. I lost my footing, too, and my grip on the stalactite and dropped down, down . . . *I knew I was going to die* . . . I tried to reach bottom with my feet to push off, but got nothing. I gulped for air, but got water. My arms flailed at my sides as I tried to pull myself up to the surface. Was this it? Was this how . . . how . . . ? No . . .

My head finally popped above the surface. I gulped for air and kept pushing off the bottom to keep from going under again. Down I went and then up. Up came the water and then down. I lifted my arms and grabbed hold of another stalactite close to the entrance of the cave, hung on tight, and willed myself out . . .

FOURTEEN

I WAS SITTING ON A CHAIR in the hospital waiting room. Buddy sat on a sofa nearby, cracking his knuckles over and over. I was shaking, even though I was trying hard not to. My clothes underneath the blanket I was wrapped in were still wet. I was still cold, too, chilled to the bone, but lucky to be alive. We were both lucky, Beanie and me.

I kept seeing pictures. Beanie sprawled facedown on the beach, shuddering until I thought her bones would crack. Ivan pumping her arms to help expel water from her lungs. Augie racing down the beach to find somebody with a cell phone. Park rangers, paramedics . . .

I saw pictures of myself, too, sucking in air as I clung to the outside wall of the cave, then heaving myself toward the cliffs, where Jason and one of the girls were waiting to grab me.

It's early evening and the waiting area is nearly empty and very quiet. An elderly woman reads a magazine on the other side of a small end table. Every so often somebody announces something on the intercom. I'm half afraid it'll be "code blue," like on television, and people will rush to Beanie's cubicle with a bunch of equipment. Instead, Dennis and Marie appear a few minutes later. They look both somber and relieved.

Buddy and I both get up. The four of us converge in the middle of the room.

"She's fine," said Dennis. "They're just checking her over, you know . . ." He looked at Buddy and then at me, letting his gaze come to rest on Buddy.

"She's dressing," said Marie. "She'll be out in a few minutes."

I felt so sorry for them, getting a call like that and racing off to the hospital, not knowing.

"So what the heck happened out there, guys? Buddy? I hope somebody has a good explanation."

I stood there shaking in my blanket, waiting for a big hug from somebody. After a second or two, I knew I wasn't going to get one. What should I say? What should I tell them?

Buddy cleared his throat. It's so quiet now I can hear his head turn. I know he's looking at me, but I don't look back.

"Maddie," says Buddy. "Would you mind running down the hall for a soda?" He holds out a dollar and some change, and I don't really want to but I take it. "Get yourself something, too. You want anything?" he says to his parents.

They shake their heads.

I hesitate. My feet feel rooted.

"Well?" says Buddy. He gives me a look. He seems nervous and irritated and wants to get rid of me. I turn and walk slowly down the hallway.

I'm nervous the whole time I'm gone, which is only about five minutes. When I return with the soda, Beanie's dressed and out in the waiting room with everyone else. She looks pale but otherwise okay.

I feel something as soon as I enter the waiting area. It's a prickly feeling. Dennis and Marie don't look at me.

Beanie jumps up and gives me a hug. She thanks me for helping to save her. I'm still hoping Dennis and Marie will get up and we'll all have a hug together in the middle of the room. Instead, there's a collective clearing of throats. Everyone stands, and we head for the door. I don't know what Buddy's told them, but I have a bad feeling.

FIFTEEN

THE McBEANS BLAMED ME for what happened. Whatever Buddy told them, they seemed to accept it. They must have believed him. I spent a lot of time wondering what he might have said. I even made up several versions of his story, so I could see myself through their eyes and know how they came to feel as they did.

"My mother said I might have died if Buddy and Ivan didn't do what they did."

Beanie and I both had bad colds. We had to spend Sunday in bed, and we weren't much better on Monday. I sneezed and sat up, reaching for a tissue. "What exactly did she say they did?"

"Oh, you know. Grabbing my arms and pulling me out. I guess Buddy and Ivan were the ones who really did it. I can't remember it myself. It's all a big blank spot. Weird I can't remember something so important, but I really can't."

I knew how it happened all right—what a trickster your memory could be. And maybe in this case, it was a good thing.

After I'd been helped out of the water myself, Buddy's friends told me how Ivan, in a last desperate attempt, had somehow grabbed hold of Beanie's hand and hung on, then pulled her up out of the cave with help from others, even from Buddy, Mr. Courage himself.

"Here I thought Buddy hated me so much," murmured Beanie. "I always figured he'd rather have me dead than alive, and look what happened!"

Yeah, look what *almost* happened, I thought with a sickening feeling. She'd been about to go under, inches from drowning, and Buddy had done almost nothing to help pull her out. Beanie, I wanted to say. Your brother's a chump and he let you down. But I knew I wouldn't, at least not yet. She looked too happy, thrilled to pieces because her brother hadn't let her drown. Or so she thought. What a guy. What a lying cowardly chicken he'd turned out to be.

Would Ivan ever tell her the truth about what happened? I didn't know. I supposed that, unlike Buddy, he wasn't much of a bragger, or perhaps Buddy had "twisted his arm."

"Well," I said, blowing into the tissue. "It's like I've been telling you, Beanie. Who could ever hate you? You're so darn lovable. Who wouldn't just love you to pieces?"

Sick as she was, she smiled. "Oh, Maddie," she said. "I'm just me."

What I said wasn't a lie. I left that sort of thing to Buddy.

It wasn't the whole truth, either, but I figured, eventually, I would have to tell Beanie what happened. Not because I was a big snitcheroo. Not because I wanted to get back at Buddy. I would have to do it because she counted on me to tell her the truth. But when I did, I was going to make darn sure she knew it was his shortcomings, not hers, that made him hang back like a coward, arms stiff at his sides, with

Beanie about to take her last breath on earth.

Beanie's mother brought us tea and toast and soup, and also a small TV. Under different circumstances, it would've been fun. But Marie would hardly look at me. She was sweet with Beanie, but with me she did what she had to do, without much feeling at all, and I could hardly stand it. At first I tried playing sicker than I was, hoping it would make her feel sorry for me, soften her up a bit. But it didn't. *I didn't do anything wrong! I went in after her!* I wanted to scream. She should've known that about me, after all those years. Wasn't I the same girl they'd always loved? Wasn't I still sweet, and wasn't I still funny?

Maybe I didn't know her, either. Maybe knowing who somebody is is a lot more complicated than I'd ever imagined.

Sometimes Buddy stopped in to see Beanie, too. This really surprised me. How dare he show his face with me there in the room watching everything? After all, I was the one who knew all about him, who knew what he really was. Or so I figured.

But his visits made Beanie happy. "I guess he's not such a jerk after all, is he? I guess you were right, Maddie. He has changed." She said this after he'd stopped by for a game of hearts. I pretended to be reading, but I was mostly busy keeping a close eye on him. I think he forgot I was there.

"I think I'll teach you to swim, Beanie. When you're up and feeling better," he said on one visit.

I looked up from my book. He blushed. I frowned. It must be a trick, a joke, and I waited for the punch line, the mean part. But there wasn't one. Just when you thought you had somebody figured out, he had to do something like that.

"Too bad it didn't work out for you two," Beanie said later.

"Yeah, too bad," I said sadly. I thought about his throwing his dog over the side at the quarry. And the shack full of what had to be stolen bicycles. I missed his special attention and how sweet he could sometimes be. And I missed almost having a boyfriend. Maybe I should've been sad about Buddy, too, that nobody was helping him out, pushing him to become the good guy he maybe could be. But I wasn't. I was too angry and disappointed and hurt.

By Tuesday evening my cold was better and I had a taste for something beside soup and crackers. I did not see Buddy standing in front of the open refrigerator when I went downstairs for a snack, grabbing an orange from the basket of fruit on the kitchen table. He turned. I looked up. We hadn't been alone since Saturday.

With the orange in my hand, I made a move to scamper from the kitchen like a little dog. I was in my sweats. My hair was a mess. Then I just stopped myself. *Whoooaaa,* said a voice in my mind. *Aren't you going to say anything?*

I watched in silence as Buddy removed a carton of milk from the top shelf and began pouring it into a glass. I heard the milk slurp and gurgle as it hit the bottom of the glass and watched it rise quickly to the top.

"What did you tell them?" I asked.

"Tell who?" he replied, without turning or lifting his head. He reached for a yellow sponge and began to wipe down the counter.

"Your parents. What did you say? What'd you tell them about what happened?"

"Maddie, it's really none of your business, what I told them." He stopped what he was doing and turned. "If you were as smart as you are cute, you'd lay off and butt out right now. This isn't your family."

It was hard to hear it said like that, out loud and right to my face. It wasn't my family. He was right about that, and I could've cried right there on the spot, but I had more to say. I took a deep breath, but my voice was still shaky.

"But I know you didn't tell them the truth. You made up some story, and it has to do with me. I know you lied about me, so it is my business."

"You don't know anything, so just knock it off."

"I suppose you didn't say your sister would've drowned if it hadn't been for Ivan and that I . . ."

"Madison, I really wish you hadn't said that."

I started and turned. Marie was standing in the doorway, hands clasped tightly together in front of her. My mouth fell open.

"Ma . . . Marie," I stuttered. "But he . . . he . . ."

"I'm so disappointed," she quickly interrupted. "Dennis and I expected a lot more from you, Madison. What were you thinking? You know Beanie can't swim. You should've used your head out there. And here you are, stirring it all up again, after what almost happened."

It was the first scolding I'd had from her, ever. I wanted to hang my head and start bawling my eyes out. But I held my head up; in my heart, I knew I didn't deserve it. I knew it was a lost cause, too, but I had nothing to lose, so I turned to Buddy. "Why don't you just tell her what really happened? Tell her the truth, Buddy, for once in your life. Please."

He tilted his head back and drank, slowly, while I waited, my heart thumping hard in my chest. I knew he was stalling, thinking, maybe, I hoped, digging deep inside himself to find the courage to do the right thing. When he'd downed the last drop, he set the glass on the counter. "I did tell the truth," he replied flatly, wiping his mouth with the back of his hand.

I blinked hard, because I knew that was my last chance. Nothing would ever be the same again, not with the McBeans, not in this lifetime.

"Marie," I said, turning to face her. She looked so tired. Her eyes were full of a sad disappointment. Was it really disappointment in me? I wondered. Or had she begun to have doubts about Buddy?

"I didn't . . . It didn't happen the way he said. You could ask somebody who was there, Ivan or Augie . . ." My voice broke.

"Buddy doesn't lie," she solemnly replied.

"Yes, Buddy does lie," I said. Before I could say more, I felt my face begin to crumple and hurriedly slipped past her. Maybe Beanie was right. Maybe they were stupid after all.

On Wednesday morning I told the McBeans I wanted to go home early. I couldn't see spending the last few days trying to win back their approval. I didn't have the heart for it, and they'd never choose me over Buddy, anyway. I was hoping they would stop me, though, or want to talk things over together like the old times. But the McBeans didn't seem to mind the idea at all. So I called my folks early that evening.

There we were, Beanie and her parents and me at the airport three days early. "Thanks for everything," I murmured to Dennis and Marie. I was very polite. We were all very polite, right down to the exchange of a very polite and germ-free hug that lasted about three-quarters of a second.

Saying good-bye to Beanie was another story altogether, a gut-wrenching moment I'd been dreading all day. As we stepped away from her parents, I still hadn't told her the truth about her brother. She still seemed fragile to me, and I didn't want to make a mistake. I didn't know if waiting to tell her was the right thing or the wrong thing, or if I should tell her at all. Was I lacking in courage or trying too hard to protect her? If I didn't tell her, could something terrible happen again? It was all a big confusing jumble in my head, and I'd decided to talk it over with my parents at home.

"I wish you weren't going," said Beanie.

I nodded, my eyes welling up.

"I wish I was going back with you."

"So do I. When you do come, we'll have a great time hanging out at all the old places, just like we used to do. And don't forget everything I said." I told her again how she was really a great person and how lucky I was that she was still alive, because I planned on having her as a best friend for a very long time. Then I hoisted my backpack up onto my back, threw my arms around her neck, and turned to go.

Beanie was still standing off by herself when I took a last look as I went through the gate. Though I didn't fully understand it all yet, I knew in that moment, deep in my heart, that her parents were failing both their children in a way that mine would never fail me. The McBeans always had failed their children, and they would go right on failing them in the days and years to come. *I* was the one who was lucky, not Beanie.

I gazed out the cabin window at the flat open spaces of the Midwest far far below, a vast sea of wheat and corn and potato fields no matter where you looked. Not one person had told me I'd done a brave thing by going in after Beanie that day at Sculptured Beach. I found this ironic. Here I'd spent half my childhood trying to impress the McBeans, and after doing the very thing that should've earned me a gold medal of approval, I'd lost them.

Life was funny, because even after the biggest act of bravery in my life, next to going in after Mambo, flying still made me nervous. I could still feel afraid. But maybe it was okay to say that, even okay to feel it, as long as I wasn't the one flying the plane.

The Worriers will be waiting for me at the gate, along with my sister, Ginger. They'll be early, so as not to be late. It's 3:15 but they may have arrived at the airport in time for lunch, maybe a grilled cheese sandwich or a burger and fries.

Keeping to family tradition, when I tell them the whole story, they will give me plenty of advice. They'll tell me to try not to take what happened too personally. They'll tell me how hard it is for parents to be good parents and that someday the McBeans will probably know what really happened.

My parents usually try to see the good side of people. I

like that about them, but I wasn't sure they were right about the McBeans.

Buddy had fooled his parents for a long, long time, and I didn't see much sign of its changing. This was something I did not like about the McBeans. Thinking your own kid can do no wrong. Blaming somebody else for what your own kid has done. They were not bad people, but I'd admired them so much for so long, I couldn't figure out how I was supposed to feel about them now.

It left me with a lot to think about, including why the first boy I liked turned out to be such a big loser. Somewhere inside me, I'd known it all along. Why hadn't I followed my intuition? It was something I was going to wonder about for a long time. But I knew what it was that really bothered me about Buddy. I didn't mind that he'd been so afraid that terrible day at Sculptured Beach. I minded that he passed himself off as somebody who wasn't.

I was somebody who was—afraid of a lot of things, that is. Going off to high school was just one of them. But I was lucky. I was going home to parents who would give me the kind of send-off I needed. They'd probably want to smother me in the next few weeks, and I'd probably let them. In fact, as we taxi down the runway and I grab my things from under the seat, I feel like a human sponge, ready to soak up every morsel of concern, affection, and understanding that will come my way. I know there will be plenty. I only wish I could share it with Beanie.